ACCEPTABLE LIMITS

A GRUMPY ROCK STAR ROMANCE

Olivia Sinclair

*For all current and future members
of the UNglued*

1

TODD

Damn boat drinks like a deprived alcoholic on shore leave. I watch the old-fashioned counter on the marina gas pump flip rapidly over and over, slowing ever so slightly after it crests $5,000. And that's just a top up. The gas gauge was sitting at about 3/4 when I decided it might be a good idea to fill the tank.

A few seagulls take to the air, screaming in outrage. I'd like to think it's over gas prices and inefficient fuel consumption, but it probably has more to do with the salmon guts one of the line fishermen just tossed over the pier. A late-afternoon breeze blows in the salty tang of the water and creosote pilings mixing with the fuel fumes. It's a smell that makes you feel alive even if it's never going to be a billboard signature scent. I grimace wryly, thinking about the last image consultant that tried to talk me into being the face of some noxious chemical brew masquerading as cologne. That conversation lasted only as long as it took me to press the elevator button. I don't miss that kind of shit, not even a little. When Unspeakable Noise gave up touring it got even easier for me to say no to all the side hustles.

But every time I think about selling Bianca, something comes up that makes me glad to have a fast and reliable way to travel over the water. An emergency trip for someone into Seattle or for the first time in what seems like forever, a really hot date with a woman I'd like to impress.

I could down-grade to something smaller, and a little more efficient, but I need a better handle on how I'd be using it first. So mostly I glare at Bianca's graceful white curves, wish she wasn't quite so needy, and hand my credit card over to Frank, the grizzled owner/manager of the bait shop and gas station.

The beautiful thing about Frank is that he doesn't ask questions. Just runs my card and hands it back without a murmur or even making eye contact. If only I could believe his clamped lips would stay that way. Except that Frank and my Uncle Lou are best buds. They gossip like teenage girls when they think nobody can hear them. And their hearing is going fast, both of them, so there's no getting it through their thick heads that what they can't hear, the rest of the island *can*.

Which is why I waited until the last minute to top up the boat, and to ask Lilah out... which I still haven't done yet. The clock on my phone says I'd better get a move on. She'll be starting her close-up routine in about twenty minutes. I hope she's not too pissed that I'm not giving her days of warning. I want to make this special for her and having the entire island whispering is not my idea of fun. So short notice, but I've got a table at the best restaurant in Seattle, one where celebrities are commonplace and the service is practically invisible.

I've gone as slowly as I possibly can with her because she's not a quick fuck and I want to make it clear to her that I'm after so much more than that. Plus, I'll flatten the first person who suggests she's anything but precious. I haven't even kissed her yet, which is downright shocking when you consider that she's been starring in every single one of my x-rated fantasies for the last six months.

Never thought I'd find someone like Lilah here, not in a million years. It took me a few months just to accept that she wasn't a figment of my imagination. I'd pretty much expected to live out my days as a grumpy bachelor, much like Uncle Lou, and definitely not making long-term plans with someone as young as Lilah.

The age difference still makes me nervous. Most of the women I've encountered in their twenties couldn't spend more than a minute or two on an actual conversation. And definitely not on one unrelated to diets, clothes, or sex interspersed with whatever the vacuous word of their generation happens to be. Admittedly, most of the ones I've encountered were somehow associated with the entertainment industry and desperately hoping to be discovered. But in my jaded opinion, once a woman gets into her thirties, she goes one of two ways and it's wise to know which way she's headed before getting involved, even platonically.

Either she sinks back into the bitchy rules of high school and ratchets that up several notches or she finds the nerve to shed that shit completely and finally speaks her mind. That latter group has the women I prefer to spend time with, even if it's only for one night of mutual pleasure.

But Lilah's got an old soul, an incredibly sharp mind, and the sweetest ass I've ever seen on a woman of any age. I want her attention on me for more than twenty minutes a day over a cup of coffee. Coffee I never used to drink in the afternoons, but what the hell else am I going to find as a regular excuse to visit the owner of a coffee shop when she's free to chat?

I need more of her. I need *all* of her. And I want her to want more of me. I'd also like to be close enough to grab that ass first thing in the morning and sink my aching cock into her tight pussy before I make *her* coffee. Just thinking about her lounging naked in my bed, her caramel hair mussed while she closes her eyes over those first few sips, has me getting hard. I glance around the main cabin of the boat and take a quick peek in the head and the lounge below, just to make sure everything looks presentable. I haven't had Bianca out for more than an engine check in months, so it might be a little dusty, but everything looks fine.

Time to put her back in her berth for a few hours and finally make a move on my girl.

LILAH

It's almost closing time. I nervously smooth the skirt of my bright yellow summer dress down with damp hands. It's a little late in the season for this outfit, but it's one of my favorites and I cling to the reminder of warmer weather for as long as possible. Even if it means shivering slightly when the wind picks up off the harbor.

I make those same hands start gathering up the little ceramic boxes for sugar packets so I can refill them at the counter, ready for tomorrow. Shortly after I arrived on the island, I tried to introduce actual sugar bowls with less refined turbinado sugar, but there was basically a rebellion. Nobody wanted sweetener that didn't come from a little paper packet. Not in this town. And they all, to a man, woman, and child, want their drinks as sweet as they can get away with. I go through a lot of sugar packets.

My hips swivel instinctively to the classic rock on the radio playing softly over the sound system while I stuff new packets into the thick, white containers.

But I digress. It's not sugar that has me anxiously looking out the plate-glass door towards the harbor. I saw Todd's lanky form heading purposefully towards the marina almost an hour ago. I don't know if that means he's skipping his usual afternoon coffee or stopping in for that on his way home. He's... I can't quite figure out how to describe him. He's got that thing, where you instantly stop and turn when he comes into a room and yet he does absolutely nothing to command that attention.

Todd's more intellectual than brash. I wouldn't call him shy, not at all, but he's... I guess he's got more confidence than anyone I've ever met, so it doesn't have to bleed into arrogance. He just is, and he accepts everyone else as they come. He doesn't go out of his way to smile. Usually his face is somewhat stern and expressionless, but his eyes always seem warm to me. And how can eyes be any temperature? Surely that's just my imagination attempting to entertain me.

Although Todd is definitely hot. Did I mention that? He's not brawny or skinny, but that perfect spot in between. And graceful like a panther when he moves. I think he likes me, just a little, in a personal way. But I've been wrong about that kind of thing before, so I'm no judge. Just every now and then, I get a little hint. A tiny quirk of his lips as if he can't help being amused by me or the light touch of his fingers as he takes his coffee cup. Sometimes his gaze seems to linger on my lips, which always makes me feel like I ought to say something clever.

But I can't come on to a customer. I mean, I don't think I've got the nerve to come on to anyone really, not without a lot of positive encouragement from the come-on-ee. But I really don't want to make the wrong assumption if all he's truly here for is the coffee and a little conversation to break up his day.

Of course, there is the way he keeps trying to tip with hundred-dollar bills, but always in a way that he thinks I won't catch him at it. I'll turn my back and he'll try to slip a bill down into the bottom of the tip jar by the register. But seriously, who else in this town has that kind of money? Particularly in the off-season.

He was some kind of producer in LA or something like that, but you'd never know it from how he acts. He's completely down to earth except for those damn hundred-dollar tips. Whenever I try to confront him, he gives me one of those disdainful looks with a raised eyebrow that has me feeling like I've made up something for an excuse to talk to him. But there's always a muted twinkle in his eyes that invites me to share the joke. I'm so confused I don't know what's going on anymore.

I know he's quite a bit older than my twenty-six years, but I kind of like that. I think that's part of why he seems so in control without being anal. That confidence again. A man my age would be pushing for a date, then pushing for sex on the first date. I don't think Todd's like that. I'm positive he's not lacking in that department, but I suspect he may favor quality over quantity. Or I'm completely off base and he's got a wife and six kids on the mainland and isn't interested in me at all. Sigh.

Of course, just as that thought hits, I see him striding straight down the sidewalk towards the Embraceable Brew (my aunt came up with that name, so don't blame me). I hurriedly duck back behind the counter and try to act like I wasn't staring down the street looking for him. I can't hold back my smile though when he opens the door or stop myself from saying a cheerful, "Hiya."

His rich brown eyes smile at me, but his face stays serious. "Hey, Lilah. I'm not too late, am I?"

"You? Never. I'm just keeping busy with the flood of customers." I mock roll my eyes around the empty cafe. "You want your usual?"

"Sure, why not?" He opens his mouth like he's about to add to that short sentence and I wait, my brows raised, one hand on the espresso machine. But a moment later, his perfect lips close again and he sort of shakes his head like he's trying to clear it. So I turn back to make his simple drink. Todd is the one customer that doesn't dump sugar or syrup in his drinks, so they're relatively quick to make.

"You don't need to keep tipping like that, you know," I scold him without turning around. I can see him in the shiny reflection of the stainless steel — well enough to follow his movements.

He just smiles politely when I finally turn around to see why he's being so quiet. I half-expected guilt but… yeah, guess that's not an emotion he spends much time with.

I hand him his drink and shake my head firmly when he reaches for his wallet. "Not on your life. You've got about six thousand more of those coming before you're allowed to pay. And that's only if you knock off those ridiculous tips."

He rolls his eyes at me while leaning against the counter. I go back to basically pretending to wrap up for the afternoon. My right hand is still tingling where his fingers brushed it when I handed him his cup. I frantically remind myself that this is just a spot of light amusement in his afternoon. The butterflies in my stomach are just my normal reaction to his charisma. It's not a relationship or about to turn into one. It's just a hot older guy getting coffee every single day. A drink that he absently sips while his eyes track my movements around the bright interior of the coffee shop.

I inherited the place from my aunt a year ago. She had it built in an extra modern Northwest style, with lots of glass and heavy wood beams. It's beautiful and takes a cleaning crew of three people at least four hours to keep those windows sparkling every week. I think it was more of a hobby for Aunt Nina than a bottom-line business, so I kind of doubt she factored in things like cleaning costs when she was planning it.

I'm unusually antsy with nerves for some reason, more so than normal when Todd's here. So when my least favorite song in the world comes on the radio, I grimace and bend down to hit the off switch. I can't take the song about a green-eyed witch (everyone knows they wanted to say bitch, really) on top of everything else.

"Not a UN fan, huh?" Todd asks with amusement from the counter.

I blink as I stand up. What does the United Nations have to do with… oh, he means the band. "Um no? Not really. A little before my time, but I hate that song with a passion." And I'm so not part of their in-crowd as to use the shortened version of the band's name Unspeakable Noise, despite all their cutesy album names that start with the acronym.

Todd's looking at me a little funny when I finally stand up straight and turn towards him. Oh no, does he like that one? It doesn't seem like his kind of thing at all. "My bus driver in third grade played it on an endless loop. Said it kept everyone in line," I explain and his eyes widen.

"Wow. I hadn't heard it was used as torture on small children."

I smile in response. "Totally was. But I'm sure those guys don't care anymore. They must be ancient by now. Probably chasing nurses half their age around the retirement home trying to recapture their youth." I absently wipe down the counter one more time, trying to figure out why I'm so nervous. This isn't any different from any other Friday when Todd's stopped in, or any other weekday, for that matter. In the off-season, I close the coffee shop on the weekends. There just isn't enough local traffic to justify keeping it open. And not nearly enough on the weekdays either. One more thing to worry about.

When I come around to the part of the counter where Todd is, he's frowning down at his phone. "Everything okay?" I ask, wondering why he suddenly seems even more closed off.

He looks up, his eyes softening slightly as they meet mine. "Yeah, just realized I need to cancel an appointment, and it took me a minute to find the right spot on the site. Don't know why people can't talk to each other anymore."

"Yeah, I know what you mean." Okay, I don't, not really. Having a phone surgically attached to me has been a normal part of my life since middle school.

But that doesn't mean I think it's a good idea or that I don't understand the culture shock of previous generations that came to it later in life (and who I blame for inventing the darn things in the first place.)

"Can I help you put up the chairs for the cleaners?" Todd asks casually, sliding his phone into his back pocket.

"Have I ever said no?" I tease him gently. It's not that it's all that much work, but I appreciate having company with such a mundane end of the day chore.

He starts upending chairs onto the tabletops, leaving the floor clear for the solid mopping Kristy and her crew will deliver in a few hours. Todd manages two chairs for every one I do, so it's all done in no time. I live in the tiny apartment over the back that I can access through the small office at the rear of the shop. So when all the chairs are up, Todd walks me to the front door and exits, giving me an oddly searching glance as he steps over the threshold. But as always, he waits for me to lock the door behind him. He read me the riot act one time when I didn't do it right away, saying that was the time frame when someone was most likely to expect me to be alone and defenseless. He's right, but this is Embrace Island, winter population of about 5,000 souls. It's not exactly the center of a crime wave.

But I had to acknowledge Todd's point that drug addiction spared no part of the country, rural or city, and a junkie on the island had fewer opportunities for more benign crimes to acquire cash. I didn't enjoy the reality check, but I appreciated that he was more worried about me than about being polite. It's nice that he cares. I just wish he would show that caring in a more personal, just for me, possibly naked kind of way. I sigh as I shut off the lights and head to the back, double checking that door is locked too and head upstairs to my little haven. Alone, just like always.

TODD

The narrow street nearest the harbor is mostly dark now, only illuminated by two dim streetlights on either end. Winter is moving in fast, which means the sun's gone down long before the extra-curricular school bus does its meander around the island while parents wait at the end of driveways with welcoming flashlights. When I first moved back to the island, I thought it was some kind of weird religious ritual until someone explained it to me. I think my version is more poetic, and it's still hanging at the back of my mind for some future project.

I linger at the corner until I see Lilah's light come on at the rear of the building. I don't like her living down here all by herself. None of the other shops or businesses have residential units attached, so it's pretty empty once things close. And at this time of the year, half the businesses don't bother opening at all. They'll hibernate like bears and come roaring back to life in mid-April.

Lilah prides herself on her independence. She still hasn't told me everything about how she came to be running a coffeehouse on Embrace Island, but what little she has shared points to courageous through and through.

There's nothing to be gained by standing out here like a stalker at this point. I need to take a step back, reassess, and figure out a new path to my goal. It's a contemplative walk back up the hill to my monstrosity of a house. The fact that I'm living in it is beyond ironic and reminds me of how foolish I was in my youth. When I was about the same age Lilah is now, I admit to myself with an eye roll. But she'd never have something like that built. She's too smart and has far too good taste. I couldn't care less that she isn't a UN fan, or that she hates the single that put us on top of the charts for a solid year and paid for the silly house. It's not a particularly great song. When we're really feeling honest, every member of the band can admit it's sappy, over the top, teenage shit. Shit that continues to sell really, really well.

But I hadn't taken into account that she doesn't know who I am, even without the tattoos. Most of the lifelong residents know, but they don't talk about it. Either because they remember me from the two years my mom and I lived with my uncle when I was a little kid or they overhear him talking at the top of his lungs about God knows what I've given him most recently 'wasting my damn fool money' and don't want to get dragged into that.

I also hadn't anticipated that she'd consigned me to the geriatric age group. There isn't too much in common between the public image of the band's lead singer and me, except there's no denying we share a birthday. So even though Lilah didn't associate me with the rock star persona, and a lot of off-islanders don't without the ink, she flat out told me I was too old for her. Ancient doesn't exactly imply someone she's willing to date. So maybe I've misread the signals and let my ego see something that isn't there? Damn it, I hate feeling like a cliché.

Whatever I saw in her eyes and reflected in her warm smile couldn't be what I thought it was. Probably time I got my eyes checked for glasses. Fuck it all. I need to take a bigger step back because the last thing I want to do is pressure her into something she's not completely enthusiastic about. And I'm really not clear on how to start the conversation that clues her in as to who I am away from the island without sounding like an ass and scaring her off. And all before someone else does it for me.

I trudge up the steepest part of the hill in the pitch dark, navigating half by memory and half by peculiarly good night vision. I'm distracted enough, though, that I almost miss the big pothole that the town refuses to fill in. I catch myself just in time, make a mental note to call someone to fix it since nobody else is going to care enough, and finally unlock the side door of my ridiculously flashy mansion. Alone. Not exactly the homecoming I was hoping for.

2

LILAH

It takes me a few days before I finally accept that Todd is avoiding me. Of course, I missed him when I didn't see him on Monday, particularly after I spent the entire weekend feeling restless and out of sorts. But I figured he had something more important to do. On Tuesday, I thought that maybe he'd caught a cold or was out of town for a long weekend.

Then it occurred to me I'd simply missed him because I found another hundred-dollar bill in the tip jar. I thought maybe he'd stopped in when I ran to the bank and left my shop neighbor, Missy, in charge for those five minutes. But Missy swears she didn't see anyone matching his description.

When the tips keep appearing and on days when I never leave the cafe, I finally admit something has changed. And not in a good way. Did I say something wrong? Did he, God forbid, realize I was lusting after him and wanted nothing more to do with the crazy woman at the only coffee shop in town? I have no idea.

I do plan to track him down and ask just as soon as I can formulate a coherent question. Because right now all I want to do is cry until he pulls me close and kisses me into next week. Thus confirming the crazy diagnosis if he was leaning that direction. Quite simply, I miss him.

I make an effort to figure out who's leaving the tips because maybe they know something that will clue me in. But after a week I'm forced to acknowledge that it's several people. Does he need to avoid me that badly that he's made up an entire plan? Something aches deep inside when I think about him not wanting to see me. And why does he keep sending me money if that's how he feels? I'm ashamed to admit that the extra cash is staving off the inevitable.

I don't see how I can keep the shop open past the end of the year unless some miracle comes along. And I'm not interested in one shaped like a sugar daddy. But it turns out that's what my aunt was to her own business. Since I was moping over Todd anyway, I finally dragged out the files from the storeroom. I've avoided going over the old books because I knew they would depress me.

But I'm actually doing better at running the business than my aunt was. Except she was floating it with large cash infusions from her retirement savings.

And why not? From the sounds of it, she loved talking to people and being part of the community. But when she left the shop to me, her money was mostly gone and was split between other relatives, anyway. And I don't have a reserve like that to draw from. Or at least not much, and that's my survival fund if I need to pack up and find a regular job on the mainland. Which is looking increasingly likely.

Blurry-eyed from the sheer sense of failure in all aspects of my life, I glance up blindly and spot a familiar gait moving past the door. I half raise my hand in greeting and then awkwardly lower it again when I realize Todd isn't looking this way. I try to swallow past the lump in my throat. What the fuck happened? He doesn't strike me as the passive aggressive type. If I said or did something to piss him off, I'd expect him to tell me about it. Like he did when he gave me hell for not locking up. I just don't get it.

It takes three more days for the rest of the pieces to fall into place. Three very lonely days because business is pretty much nonexistent. I'm talking two or three customers a day, which doesn't even pay for the sugar packets they stuff in their pockets to use later. Mind you, at least one of them manages to drop in yet another hundred-dollar bill in the tip jar. I should just sign the deed over to Todd and call it good. But that would mean finding the man. I've been looking as much as I can without leaving the shop unattended for more than ten minutes.

Yes, I left a business wide open and unsupervised (several times) and absolutely nothing happened, probably because my stomach was already filled with dread at facing Todd's rejection. So how much worse can things get? Plus, the harbor area is so dead these days nobody even tried to walk out with sugar while I was gone.

I'm scrubbing down spotless tables one more time — nothing gets dirty if nobody uses them — when my friend Bethany comes bursting through the door, her red curls flying, a grin on her freckled face, and waving a copy of the inter-island gazette over her head. "It's an omen, Lilah!"

"What is?" I smile in response, because she's just one of those people that can cheer up a funeral home without even trying.

"Well… first of all, we made the front page of the Gazette, and you know that never happens."

I gape in shock. It seriously never happens. The Gazette is an almost-no-budget local paper that covers ten islands. Naturally the headlines, and quite frankly the next two or three pages, get reserved for the island where the newspaper office is, and after that it's pretty much in descending order of both population and advertising dollars. Both of which put

Embrace Island scraping the bottom, hoping for a mention in 'Other Island News' on the last page.

"What the hell happened?" I try to grab Bethany's arm so I can get a look at the paper, but she's taller than me and immediately puts it out of my reach.

"*That's* the other excitement. I think this could save your business." I frown at that. That's asking a lot — way more than the Gazette can deliver, even on the front page.

"Well, what is it?" I ask skeptically.

Bethany spreads the paper out with a flourish on the table I was just wiping. "Unspeakable Noise is reuniting. Here on Embrace Island. Can you believe it?" Her voice rises to such a shriek of excitement I have to hold my hands to my ears.

"Why would they... Oh. Fuck. No." I back away from the table in horror my hand slapped to my mouth.

"Babe?" Bethany is looking at me like I'm watching invisible aliens that she can't see. In a way, maybe I am. I point down to the photo on the front page of the paper — the one where five heavily tattooed guys lean against the railing of a marina in studied casual poses.

"That's Todd. Why is Todd with those guys? Why does he have tattoos? Todd doesn't have tattoos. None that I know of, anyway. Definitely not like *that*."

"Okaaay. Yeah, that's Todd Kipling, lead singer of UN. You knew that, right, hon? Pretty much everyone and their grandma gets that one right on trivia night."

I shake my head violently. I didn't. I didn't know it at all. My stomach roils as the final pieces of the puzzle click into place. "I've screwed up, Bethy. Really, really bad."

"You need a special mocha?" she asks softly, her eyes kind.

I nod, my eyes pleading. "Yes." That comes out in about three syllables because I'm already starting to ugly cry.

Bethany briskly moves to the front door, locks it and switches the sign over to closed, then moves behind the counter. Our special mocha involves the same milk and chocolate syrup, but also has a stiff shot of rum. Which I don't have a license for and which I don't serve to customers, but I do keep squirreled away for dire emergencies. This definitely counts.

At least I now know why Todd hasn't been in. Bethany's a good friend and she doesn't press. I can tell she's curious but she keeps the conversation light, talking about the shopping district's plans for Christmas decorations which are going to have a sea creature theme this year. Because nothing says happy holidays like crabs and starfish. (Oh, goody! *Not*).

While she talks, I sip my drink and try to recover my equilibrium. When I can breathe steadily again, I pull the paper over to me so that I can attempt to learn what apparently everyone else already knew. It's hard because the Gazette doesn't actually pay any reporters, so it reads more like a high-school English essay, but I do learn a few things. The group is getting together for studio sessions only — to release a new album. There are no plans for a tour. The photo on the front was from three years ago. Only one band member lives on the island and the rumor is all this album stuff will happen at his house. Starting sometime in November. I glance at the date of the paper. It's a biweekly, and it usually takes a week to get here. Yep, all the other islands already know. And November starts next week. So if I'm going to catch Todd alone before I have to pack up the tatters of my pride and my nonexistent business, it's going to have to be soon. I owe him a sincere apology, not excuses, which means I don't have the right to ask for anything in return. Not even his friendship.

"Do you know where Todd lives, Bethy?" I finally ask quietly. Maybe it's false courage from the alcohol but I'm proud of myself for facing my mistakes.

"Umm. I think up on the ridge, you know back behind the rim road where the cliffs are? One of those big fancy houses that face the ocean. All of those guys are worth millions, but he has the most song credits, so I think he's worth even more. His uncle lives here in town, so I guess that's why he stays."

Yeah, definitely no room to ask for anything, like having my friend back. Billionaire rock stars aren't friends with failing coffee shop owners. Not unless they're fucking them on the side and he definitely hasn't made that kind of move.

"I thought he was a Hollywood producer," I sadly confess to Bethany.

"You weren't too far off," she says cheerfully, clearly trying to bolster my spirits.

"You weren't here. I don't even remember half the things I said to him because I was nervous talking, but it was bad."

"Doesn't mean you can't sell the fans coffee though, does it?"

"Nooo, but are people actually going to come here? I... they're not even performing publicly, are they?"

"The die-hards won't miss a chance for a surprise sighting. They call themselves the *UNglued* and they kinda mean it."

I snort-gurgle through my tears. "Who comes up with all those sort-of-puns?"

Bethany regards me like she might a wild animal

that is acting strange. "I think someone probably has a dictionary. Why?"

I shake my head. It doesn't matter, really. Maybe an influx of Unspeakable Noise fans can prolong closing for a little while and maybe they can't. I have to make plans now for the worst-case scenario, and that includes tracking down Todd by the end of the week.

TODD

Fuck. I do not have time to deal with the guys right now. Or their damn need to shoot the breeze over beers every three hours. I need to get Lilah back. Hell, I need to get Lilah for the first time before this all blows up in my face, so I stand a chance of getting her back then.

The band wasn't supposed to be here until next week. That's what we agreed to. But no, Karl, Ernest, and Roman all decided they wanted to get in some vacation time first and showed up two days ago. That just leaves Lance, and God only knows when he'll drift in. Right when it's most inconvenient is usually the way it goes.

Any other time I'd love to catch up, well... after an hour of hearing about Roman's new love of organic gardening, I've had about enough. But I'm happy he's found something he enjoys that doesn't involve people trying to suck him dry. Despite rumors to the contrary, the band did not break up over any love triangles or drug overdoses or managers stealing money. The band broke up because to a man we all hated touring. And when I finally put my foot down and said I was done, everyone else shrugged indifferently and agreed. We "reunite" when there's a reason to, but we do it without involving a tour bus. Guaranteed in a month or two, there will be stories about infighting or something.

This time Ernest's mom needs to go into a nursing home, permanently. Which really sucks because I remember her as the mom that never complained about the banging of drums in her garage. And she always brought out sandwiches to a bunch of boys that were just old enough to realize there wasn't much money in that house and still young enough to be in a constant state of near starvation. She was awesome, so to hear that she needs daily assistance is just sad. And Ernie won't take the money from any of us after some of his investments went south so that she can go into a top of the line facility but he will take another album. So here we are. I'm in the kitchen trying to figure out how to win Lilah and they're acting like teenagers in the big sunken living room, catching up on not much of anything.

There's a business-like rap on the door and I get up to see who it is. I don't get many visitors out this way. Largely because I'm an antisocial bugger but also because there just isn't that much business to conduct on the island and usually I go to them so they don't get intimated by this stupid house.

Kristy, the cleaning lady, is standing with military-perfect posture on the stoop. Which makes her sound like a fifty-year-old worn-out matron. In reality, she's not too much older than Lilah, and I know she did three tours in the army before coming back to take care of her grandmother. She's endlessly capable and fit, but that doesn't mean I don't send a nervous glance into the living room.

When the guys get together, they tend to revert to high school and none of us were exactly smooth with women back then. *Or now*, I amend to myself trying to figure out why I can't just throw Lilah over my shoulder and keep her until she agrees that's where she belongs. I don't need the guys pissing Kristy off by coming on to her or saying something obnoxious in her presence.

"Hey, Todd."

"Hi, Kristy. Did you switch days or something? Sorry, I forgot if you mentioned it."

"No, you didn't forget. But you did ask me to let you know if Lilah said anything about money problems?"

I nod, concern for my girl settling into my stomach like a lead weight. I hate to see her stressing about something I could so easily fix, if she'd let me.

"She stayed late yesterday to let me know she couldn't keep me on after this week. She said she'd either be out of business or in better shape at the end of November."

"Fuck." I glance into the living room to make sure the guys aren't listening, but they're still busy shooting the shit and haven't noticed my visitor.

"Alright. Thanks, Kristy. Hey, are you okay without her business? I can…"

She doesn't let me finish. Instead, she issues a military-direct curt shake of her head. "Nope. I'm good. More business than I can handle anyway, but I hate to see her go down like that. Lilah's good people. I already tried earlier to offer her a reduced rate for the off-season, but she wouldn't take it."

I nod. Lilah is good people and despite not being a native to the island I've watched the old crotchety locals warm up to her like flowers turning to the sun. She might not have picked up on it because they still sound growly, but they're more cheerful growls than they used to be.

"I'll figure something out." I sigh as I walk her to the door. "Thanks for telling me, Kristy." She gives another curt nod and walks briskly to her shiny white van. I'm back to thinking the caveman strategy is the only one with any chance of success.

3

LILAH

Friday brings a few more customers in. But not so many that I don't have plenty of time to wallow in my new found guilt. Plus a not-so-healthy helping of self-pity regarding the state of the business. Now that I've confessed my lack of funds to Kristy, I feel like the end is actually happening. But before I start contacting real-estate agents (none of whom live on the island) I need to get my apology to Todd over with. Not to mention that my stomach hurts when I try to remember exactly what I said to him because the parts I do recall were pretty awful. And that probably means the rest was even worse. I don't really want to run away. I want to fix things so they can go back the way they were. But I know that's not possible. And I suppose the silver lining at least is that once I head to the mainland, I won't be running into him, even accidentally. I'm ignoring the shooting pain in my heart when I think about never seeing him again. It's for the best.

Glancing around the empty cafe, I decide I might as well close up early and go get that over with. If I head out in the next twenty minutes, I can make it to the top of the hill (the locals call it a mountain) before it gets dark. I'll say my piece and then give myself the weekend to wallow in ice cream to get over everything. I flip the open sign to closed and upend the chairs, knowing this is the last time I'll do that for Kristy's crew. After tonight, I'll have to mop up and clean the restrooms myself. At least while I still own the place. In truth, I don't really believe Bethany's theory that the ferry is going to bring hoards of UN fans to the island. It's a nice image but... seriously.

My poor little car is sitting under a half-inch carpet of fallen birch leaves. I hardly ever use it because most everything I need on the island is within walking distance. And when money started getting tight last spring, I confess car maintenance was an easy place to cut. So it's not a huge surprise that it takes me five minutes to get her started.

I tootle through the small side streets of the village, angling towards the base of the big hill. My car doesn't quite feel like she has her usual pep, but nothing's clanking, so I put it on my list of things to do before I leave the island, so I don't break down on some freeway somewhere. I pat the dash with encouragement when the grade changes, causing the engine to cough.

Then everything motorized ceases completely,

and the car rolls backwards until it's sitting flat again. This would be scarier if I had managed more than ten feet of the hill and there was other traffic. As it is, it's just annoying. I restart the car and try again. This time it makes it fifteen feet before dying again and rolling back. I stop it midway with a firm foot on the brake, but clearly this isn't going to work. It could get dangerous if this happened halfway up where there are turns and steeper sides. I let the car roll backwards again, restart it and park it off to the side, clear of the road.

But I am not giving up on my mission. Fierce determination to do the right thing and see this through fills my belly. I need to get this over with, to achieve some kind of closure on my stupid words and see Todd one last time.

My outfit isn't the best for hiking. I have my favorite yellow dress on again, for encouragement, paired with a fluffy white sweater because autumn has hit with a vengeance. At least my white tennis shoes are good for walking, but I know they won't be white for more than five seconds on the gravel road. There's still enough light, I think, to see where I'm going.

I start up the road with bravery, and a serious pep-talk. Then the rain starts pinging down, slowly at first, then gathering speed. I scurry up the road towards the overhanging trees, thinking this will provide some cover. And it does, a little, from the rain but also the daylight, unfortunately. It's much darker under the thick branches than I realized. I fish my phone out to use the flashlight feature I've only heard about but never actually used. So it takes me a minute or two to figure out where the hell the setting for that is, because of course I have no signal, so I can't just look it up.

I don't want to lose time by stopping in my tracks, so I walk as I swipe. Which is probably how I missed the giant pothole in the middle of the road. I go down hard, my phone flying from my hand like it has wings and I'm suddenly shaking like a leaf. I take a deep breath to center myself, still lying on the wet ground, the sharp pain of gravel digging into my palms.

I'm okay. Feeling around as I bring myself up to a sitting position, I scraped my knees pretty badly and might have twisted my ankle, but nothing's broken. I push myself upright and take a few tentative steps. Yep, I can walk, but it does hurt. I look around for my phone. It's gotten even darker, and the rain has intensified, making its way through the thick overhang of branches which are now dipping lower with the weight of the water. I can't see it anywhere, nor is there any light from the screen which should in theory still be on.

I'm soaked through, my dress clinging restrictively to my thighs and calves. And when I turn around, my car is out of sight. I've been walking for a while, so I have to be closer to the top than the bottom at this point. There's nothing for it but to carry on.

Hopefully, my phone landed somewhere dry where I can retrieve it in a day or so. I know — but I'm hanging on to hope here, like that damn kitten on the motivational posters.

Long before I can see a glimmer of light through the trees, I'm completely numb. Briefly I considered curling up under a tree and trying to wait it out until morning, but seriously I could die of exposure. So I keep putting one foot in front of the other, feeling my way with my feet in the gloom. When I feel a softer texture, I move back onto the road. I don't think about anything else. Just step, check, step, check.

The looming mansion appears out of nowhere, or so it seems. Only a few higher up windows are lit and there are no exterior lights at all, so it's downright menacing. I don't know whose house this is; I don't care anymore. Someone's home, I think, and they can call someone else to come get me. Or shoot me and put me out of this misery.

It seems like the last hundred feet are the hardest. Maybe it was finally seeing a destination or the hope of getting off this ankle, but it takes forever to navigate the long driveway. When I finally press the doorbell, I can't hear anything ringing inside. Is it broken? I lean on it. Still nothing.

I try knocking, but the rain is louder than any noise my fist can make. Now tears are mixing with the raindrops on my face. How could I have made it to shelter and still be out in the storm? It's so unfair. I lean on the doorbell again, practically dry heaving with desperation. Then I sink down onto the mat.

Out of nowhere my misery is interrupted when the door flies open with a whoosh and a man is shouting, "What the fuck, man? You can't call like a normal person?" Then he goes suddenly quiet and a big hard finger pokes me in the shoulder, like he's going to see if I'm done baking or not. "Yo, TK! I think you've got one of the crazies here."

"Is it LuLu?"

"Not unless she's changed beyond all recognition."

"Then just get rid of them."

Even though I'm getting pretty close to delirious, the bored tone in Todd's voice cuts straight through. And who the hell is LuLu? Is she really why he stopped coming to the cafe? But then surely he'd know her whereabouts. Wouldn't he?

Suddenly I feel stupid for even thinking he would care enough about my opinion to be offended by mere words. I'm nobody in his world. Obviously.

"Naw, man, I think you'd better come here. She don't look too good."

Authoritative footsteps sound in the cavernous house. I curl tighter into a ball, suddenly desperate not to be recognized. I just want to get away. I scrunch my eyes closed like a little kid, believing in my heart that if I can't see anything, then nobody can see me.

"Lilah? Fuck. What the hell happened to you?" Todd barks angrily but doesn't wait for a reply to his harsh words, which I'm not capable of giving, anyway. Unexpectedly, strong arms scoop me up and carry me into the warmth of the house.

TODD

Lilah feels almost weightless in my arms. Too light. Has she been eating properly? Her exposed skin is clammy and all of her is wet and cold. And she's doing a pretty good imitation of a shy gopher trying to burrow into my chest. I hold her as tight as I dare, my heart in my throat.

One of the guys, probably Karl, says something snarky along the lines of, "Hang on! I thought we'd agreed on no women. Why do you get to have one to play with?"

I can feel my girl shrink in my arms, but she doesn't lift her head. Rage fills me and I turn to glare at them over Lilah's wet hair. "She is not a fucking groupie. She's *mine* and none of you are to look at her or touch. Ever. Speak only when spoken to where she's concerned, or you can get out and not come back."

They all sit back with shocked expressions. Then the guys who've known me forever trade glances while slow, sly grins start spreading across their smug faces. They might all be over forty and covered in faded ink, but deep inside they're still ten. On a good day.

Rolling my eyes, I turn and head upstairs to the master bedroom. I need to get Lilah warm and dry, make sure nothing's broken, and then try to get her to tell me why she was on my doorstep in the first place.

It takes longer than I like to strip her out of her wet clothes and into one of my t-shirts. She isn't talking, but neither is she willing to let go of her death grip on my neck. We work out a compromise, or rather I take charge and she lets me — where I set her on the vanity in the bathroom and move one arm at a time off my neck as necessary. She's shivering hard enough to vibrate by the time I drop her soaking wet dress in the tub. I don't linger over removing her underwear. I want to. God, I'm hungry for the time to explore her sweet curves, but this isn't it. I run a soft hand towel over her to get the worst of the water and then gently tug the fresh cotton over her head. She still won't meet my gaze.

Her knees need medical attention, but what I have in the medicine cabinet is going to have to do until I can get her to the small clinic in the morning. I shift her arms so she can hang on to me while I'm bent over and start the tedious process of digging gravel and dirt out of her cuts. I can feel her tense with each tug, but she doesn't say a word. "Almost done, baby." I try to soothe her while padding a wet towel against her scrapes, hoping to float out more of the dirt. Her right ankle is swollen, but the rest of her seems in okay shape, considering everything. I need to hear it from her, though.

"Lilah, other than your knees and ankle, is anything else hurt?" She doesn't respond, just clings tighter. "I need to you say the words, love. We'll save all the other questions for tomorrow, I promise. Are you hurt anywhere else?" I make my voice as stern as I can, trying to get through to her.

There's a long pause and then a timid but clear, "No."

Fuck, she doesn't even sound like Lilah, who's usually so full of life and sass. "Alright, baby. Come on, let's get you into bed. I'm going to go get you something to eat and a hot drink. Okay?" She doesn't respond, just tightens her arms. Right. Maybe I shouldn't leave her. I carry her into the bedroom and settle against the headboard, cradling her body with mine. What the hell was she doing out in that weather?

Instead of demanding answers the way I really want to do, I slide my phone out of my pocket and call Roman. He's the most responsible one, seeing as how he has a kid and all, although not knowing about her until she was twenty-one probably isn't quite the same thing. Still, he's more likely to understand.

"Yo, why are you calling me from down the hall?" he says immediately.

"I don't want to leave her. Will you find something hot and easy to eat and bring it to my bedroom?"

There's a snort of disbelief, then a long pause. "She okay, dude? Maybe time to take her to the hospital?"

"There isn't one on the island and I'm not risking her on the water in this storm. I think she's just in mild shock. Please?"

He grunts, but I can hear him standing up. "Fine. But I get to be best man instead of one of these bozos."

It takes me a minute to follow his train of thought, but then I glance down at Lilah's wet hair starting to spring back into bouncy curls and smile. "Yeah, not a problem," I respond softly.

Five minutes later, there's a light knock on the door. "Come in," I say as quietly as I can. I think Lilah's still awake, but I don't want to startle her. Roman cautiously sticks his grizzled face around the door, then pushes it wide when he sees he's not interrupting an orgy. He sets a small tray with a mug of tomato soup and a grilled cheese sandwich down on the nightstand.

"Thanks, man."

He nods and turns to go.

"Hey, Roman? Before you go, can you grab the blanket from the bed in the closet?"

He stares at me like I've grown two heads, but he does It anyway, laying it within reach on the empty side of the bed. "You still doing that shit, TK? I know a good shrink."

I roll my eyes. "So do I. I'm fine."

Roman looks like he doesn't believe me, but instead of arguing gives me a stiff nod, glances briefly at Lilah, and makes a swift exit, shutting the door firmly behind him.

I wrap the soft gray blanket firmly around Lilah as best I can. "Lilah, baby? It's time to eat something." I can feel her shake her head against my chest in protest.

"You need to eat. Otherwise…" I try to think of a punishment that won't scare the bejeezus out of her. Ah. "Otherwise, I'm going to have to sing *that* song to you." She goes completely still and then there's a gurgle that seems to be part laughter, part groan, and part I'm not sure what. But she takes the triangle half of the sandwich I hand to her. I can feel her nibbling on it as I run my hand up and down her back in encouragement. I don't want her to shut back down, so as soon as she's eaten that I hand her the mug of soup. She holds it reluctantly, so I hum the first few bars of the intro. This time the groan is clear, but she takes a tentative sip. Then she drains the mug.

"You want the other half of the grilled cheese?" I'm pushing my luck here. She's at least had enough to keep her going for a few hours.

"You eat it," she responds softly without lifting her head, but she sounds more like her old self. My heart moves back down towards my chest. Instead of asking the million questions buzzing in my brain or kissing her senseless, which is my other instinctive need, I wrap the gray blanket more tightly around her and settle my chin on top of her head.

She's mine now and I'm going to hold her tight as long as she needs it. And then maybe just a little bit longer. If she'll let me. I don't for a moment think we're over any of the major hurdles here. I've got work to do to convince her of a future together. My arms instinctively tighten when I think about what that's going to take. I can practically feel the looming potholes in the road ahead. I don't even realize I'm growling like an angry, protective bear until Lilah shifts against me like she's trying to move away. I kiss the top of her head until she settles down again, but it doesn't relax my brain.

4

LILAH

I wake up in a dark room with an urgent need to pee. Only I can't get up. I'm completely swaddled in something and on top of someone? I half squeak in alarm.

Then it all comes rushing back. Todd. He's still holding me close, although at some point we sort of slid into a more prone position. His deep breathing suggests he's managing to remain asleep and all I can think of is how to make an escape, so I don't make a fool of myself. Again. Because I would love nothing more than for this to be real.

Except I can't extricate myself from the damn blanket. Not without jabbing him with my elbow, and even that's not a sure thing. I sigh and give in.

"Todd? Todd, wake up. I need to get up," I whisper urgently. It takes a minute, but then I sense his breathing change.

"Hmm?" He flicks on a light and blinks at me. Awake, he's gorgeous, half asleep, he's just downright adorable. His eyes are hooded and solemn, while the dim light creates deep shadows by his cheekbones. There's scruff on his chin that if I could free my hand, I would be unable to resist touching. Then he smiles and I'm devastated all over again. "Lilah," he says in his deep voice, adding rich texture to my name that I've always thought was rather ordinary.

"I need to get up," I remind him with increasing urgency.

His face switches to concern as his brain cells start connecting again. "Hang on. I want to brace you before you test that ankle." He abruptly slides me over and stands up, then helps me unwrap from the blanket before holding his hands out.

I gingerly step forward on my good leg and then try the not so good one. It will hold me, but it hurts like hell. Before I have a chance to protest, I'm being carried into the gorgeous bathroom, all blue glass tiles and white ceramic before being set down gently. "Call me when you're done."

I shiver in the chilly room since I'm only wearing a t-shirt and I'm no longer cuddled up against the human radiator formerly known as Todd.

Of course, I don't call him when I'm done. I hop back into the bedroom, determined to resuscitate the last few scraps of my pride and get out of here. Todd must sense something of my mood because he frowns before standing again and then wrapping me protectively in a fluffy bathrobe. It's way too big for me, but so cozy, I'm not complaining.

"I need coffee if I'm going to argue with you about why you need to stay here," he says blandly before opening the door and then picking me up again. Now I'm worried he can read minds and knows all the *other* thoughts about him in my head.

Automatic lighting turns on and off as we head down the hallway. "Doesn't that get annoying?" I ask, trying to distract myself from how good it feels to be in his arms.

"Hmm? Oh the lights? Yes, it does. I hate this house." He says it so matter-of-factly that I'm beyond puzzled. If he hates it, then why the hell does he live in it?

Todd deposits me gently on a bar stool by the kitchen island. Then he sets about making coffee in a French press, scrubbing at his face with one hand while he waits in front of the electric kettle for the water to boil. I let my gaze wander around the kitchen until it's caught by a name brand I never thought I'd get to see in real life. I suck in my breath and Todd glances over at *me*, one eyebrow quirked in inquiry. "You have a Bellabestia 2000," I explain with awe. "Why the hell have you been coming in to the Embraceable Brew for coffee?" He casts his gaze to the state-of-the-art espresso machine, then back to me before pouring coffee into two cups from the simple glass carafe.

"Hold that thought," he says quietly before carrying the two mugs past me and into the living room. I swivel to get off the stool, but he stops me without turning his head. "Stay there, Lilah. I'm coming back for you."

I try not to shiver at hearing those words that play right into my fantasies. Which totally goes out the window when he does indeed come back. He swoops me into his arms again before settling into a deep armchair facing the wall of windows that probably looks out to the sea when it's not pitch black outside.

Todd wraps one arm around my hips to hold me in place before handing me one of the coffee mugs. Then he takes a deep swallow from his and heaves a sigh of satisfaction followed by, "I need to be really clear here, Lilah. You're mine. I was trying to figure out how to convince you to give an old guy a chance, but now that I've held you in my arms, there's no way I'm letting you walk away. Now, what were you doing dragging the most precious person in my life through that weather last night?"

Wait. What? I gulp at the hot coffee, hoping the caffeine will help me string those sentences together into something that makes sense. Then I give up and shake my head, saying what I came here to say in the first place. "I came to apologize," I say quietly.

I shouldn't let myself be this comfortable on his lap. I don't deserve it and no matter what he says, we can't belong together. Although I admit it's a special kind of hurt to hear him say he thinks we do.

"What the fuck for?" He's genuinely bewildered and I'm back to feeling like a nobody. But even nobodies need to be accountable for their random acts of carelessness.

"For saying mean things about you and your music. It was thoughtless and pointless, and I'm truly sorry."

"Ah, so you did figure out what I am, or someone told you... I was hoping..." he muses with a slight growl. "Lilah, I don't give a fuck what you think of the band's music or the songs I wrote as a teenager. I'd rather your attention is on me. Your belief that the age gap between us is too large is what I'm most worried about."

I blink at that. Where the hell did that come from? "I never said that!" I argue emphatically. I'd have remembered telling an outright lie.

"You did. UN is a stage setup all around, but if you're convinced Todd the artist is way too old, I don't have the power to make Todd the man any younger."

I set my empty mug down. "Todd, I have no idea how old you are or how old the others are. If I said something silly about that, it was just because you guys were adults when I was a child. Yes, I know you're older than me, but I like that. It makes you seem more... settled. Until you come out with statements like that, anyway," I amend dryly. "But in the end, it doesn't really matter because obviously there can't be anything between us."

I can feel his growl under the hand I've placed against his sculpted chest. "Now, what's the problem?"

I gesture around the room. "Well, you haven't said why, but you were clearly expecting someone named LuLu. And well, you're... a megastar. I'm barely a coffee shop owner. I can't live like this. In fact, I probably can't afford to stay on the island much longer. We're from different worlds, completely. And deep down you know that too, or you wouldn't have disappeared on me."

He scrubs his hand over his face again. "Nevermind LuLu. She's not important. And I didn't disappear. I retreated to formulate a plan and figure out how to start over with you once I realized you didn't know I was famous off-island. A plan that apparently would have been all wrong, anyway. Let's go back to why you were out walking in the dark during a storm."

I duck my head slightly and sigh. "I didn't start out that way. My car wouldn't go up the hill. So I figured I'd walk the rest of the way, but then I tripped on a pothole and my phone disappeared and well, at that point I didn't have a lot of options."

"Fuck, Lilah!" he groans before pulling me tight against him. "You're killing me here and almost killed yourself. I'm taking you to the clinic as soon as it opens to get you checked out."

Then he kisses me. For a first kiss, it's remarkably commanding and self-assured. There are no questions buried in it, it's more of a beating the chest statement kind of kiss. I like it — even more than I expected to — and I've had a lot of thoughts about how Todd might kiss.

By the time his tongue is done laying down the law inside my mouth and his lips reluctantly part from mine, I'm breathing hard and really grateful for the thick material of the robe under me. Because my thighs are feeling a little wet.

It doesn't really change anything, though. Now that I've said my piece, it's time to get back to the real world. But at least now I know that he's as perfect in real life as he's always been in my fantasies. Kind of sucks, really. Leaving him behind might be much easier if he was a bad kisser. Maybe.

"I don't need to go to the clinic, but I'd appreciate a ride down to my car." I say quietly. I don't want to leave his warmth, but what kind of awkward, uneven relationship would develop if I stuck around? I can't even bear to think of him ever sitting in this chair wondering how long I'm going to overstay my welcome.

Todd frowns harder. "Clinic. I'll have someone tow your car to the garage. I thought I told you you're staying here."

I shake my head mutely, on the verge of tears because I want that and I can't have it. Todd's gaze softens, but his grip doesn't. "Keeping you, Lilah. I can see you have to get used to that concept, but I'm not stupid enough to let you get away now."

"So you're kidnapping me?" I try for a smile, but it probably comes out as more of a grimace through the tears I'm barely keeping at bay.

"Think of it more as protective custody," he states grimly, but then drops light kisses along my hairline and down my neck.

TODD

I think I might suffer actual physical withdrawal if Lilah were to leave my arms right now. I'm more than a little mad at myself for taking so long to get her here. It didn't even occur to me that she was feeling rejected by my sudden absence. Or that I could have had a couple of months of her tucked against my chest like this already and instead now I've got an audience that I don't want. I hear the masculine throat clearing from across the room just as I'm nudging aside the folds of the robe obscuring her pretty breasts, sadly still masked by my t-shirt. I don't even try to hold back the growl and my hackles only go down ever so slightly when I hear Lilah's gasp and nervous giggle. I lift my head and carefully tuck her robe more tightly around her body. For my eyes only from this point on.

I hear coffee being poured, and then Lance, king of the awkward entrance, comes into view. Staring is all I can manage. He gulps nervously, looks briefly at Lilah curled up on my lap and then away again. He keeps his gaze fasted on the far wall.

"When did you blow in?" I ask, finally giving in.

"About three hours ago. Roman let me in, said you were otherwise occupied."

I give him a warning glare, but that's not enough to stem the tide. His mouth opens and out it comes, "Did I tell you about getting that growth on my ass checked out? They finally got around to telling me yesterday it's not cancer, but now I've got to make another appointment to get the damn thing removed."

Oddly, Lilah lifts her head at this, and I see her give Lance a long, considering glance. I cringe for him and his big mouth but her face has neither disdain nor humor. She just watches him carefully, then says, "You're a nervous talker too, aren't you?"

Lance jumps and looks back down at her, surprised. Then he flushes slightly. "That obvious, huh? What do you mean, you are too?"

She nods. "I'm Lilah. I don't even know what I blurt out half the time when certain people have hidden agendas that make me anxious." Lilah digs an elbow into my ribs. It's swamped in thick fabric so it doesn't exactly hurt, but that doesn't stop my reactive response. "Hey, I had a plan, not an agenda."

Lilah rolls her eyes. "Same difference. If you had just told me who you were and how many millions you had, I'd have not even given you a second thought and certainly not insulted you."

"I told you I wasn't insulted."

By this time, Lance has sat himself down on the coffee table and leans forward with interest. "So when's the wedding?"

My "soon" collides with Lilah's "never" and we both frown.

Lance throws his head back and laughs. "This is great. Better than anything on TV and maybe now Roman will stop being so mad at me."

I sigh with frustration. "He'll stop being angry when you apologize. To Sylvie, not to him."

"Can't do that, man."

"Why the hell not? Everyone knows it was just your mouth running."

"Sylvie doesn't, and that's the way it needs to stay." He jumps up from the coffee table with nervous energy. "You two lovebirds want pancakes?"

Now it's Lilah's eyes that are wide and ping-ponging between Lance and me. "Sure," I finally answer, but mostly to get him out of the room.

When he's gone, Lilah whispers, "Who's Sylvie and what did he say to her?"

"Sylvie is Roman's daughter who he only found out about a few years ago and Lance said, well, something I'm not going to repeat but basically implying she was a groupie with particularly loose morals."

"Ouch."

I nod in agreement. Things have been uncomfortable ever since. "Lance has apologized up one side and down the other to Roman, but he won't do the same to her. Nobody knows why and Roman is still pissed on his daughter's behalf."

Lilah nibbles her lip. "There's something there."

"What do you mean?"

"His voice changed ever so slightly when he said her name. Anyway, nevermind. If we're eating pancakes before I head home, I should change out of this bathrobe and into real clothes." She looks at me expectantly.

"Not taking you home. Or rather, you're in your new home right now. I'll grab some of your clothes from your apartment when we go into town. But fine, let's go see if I have an enveloping caftan hiding in my closet somewhere."

"You're an idiot."

"Glad you're finally seeing that the money really doesn't change anything," I tease her as I show off a little by standing up with her in my arms.

"Showoff," she chides me, "you could really hurt your back doing that."

I mock-glare at her. "I've got a lot to prove to you, apparently. What's a little lower back pain?"

"So how come you don't have all the tattoos I saw in the picture?" she asks abruptly just as we reach the foot of the staircase.

5

LILAH

Todd pauses briefly at the base of the stairs and regards me with a slight quirk to his lips. "If I tell you now, all the mystery will be gone."

I roll my eyes, but I guess if he wants to keep a few things secret, I'm not in any position to poke him about it.

He insists on carrying me back to his room and straight into his closet despite my protestations that I'm feeling stronger and should try walking again.

"Not happening," he growls on repeat before setting me down gently on a twin bed set against the wall in the luxurious walk-in closet. I'm actually insanely curious to see inside the inner clothes sanctum of a rock star, but I was not at all expecting what I see in front of me.

The racks are virtually empty. One black suit and a handful of crisp white button-downs hang overhead. There are about five pairs of running shoes on the shoe rack, along with a couple of nicer leather pairs.

"I'm pretty sure you can afford clothes," I say slowly, peering into the corners to see if I missed anything.

"I grew out of buying things I don't need a while back," Todd responds with a slow smile while pulling out a drawer that at least seems to be moderately full even if it's only populated with neatly folded t-shirts. "Which is why these racks have been waiting for you. At least until we build a new house."

"Who's we?"

"You and I are now we. And you are going to stop killing yourself with worry over money and risking your health and safety by cutting corners you can't afford to cut." He says the last part sternly with a meaningful glare.

I gape at him. "How do you know…"

He raises one eyebrow and folds his arms. "How could I not know? It's not your fault, Lilah. Let the town help."

"By town, you mean you," I conclude dryly.

"If you need a committee to feel better about it, I'm sure I can rustle one up."

"No, thank you. Clothes, please." I hold out a hand, palm up, waiting for some to magically appear. Todd sighs heavily before turning to open a second drawer. He hands me a long-sleeve t-shirt and some plaid flannel pants with a drawstring. The tag is still on those. "Gift?" I ask cautiously.

He nods. "They came with an invitation to a ski weekend. That I did not accept, by the way."

I probably put too much effort into my shrug of indifference, because I'm dying to know who invited him away for a weekend and sent him pants to do it. Pretty sure only a woman would do that, but plaid? Really? "None of my business."

"Yes, it damn well is your business. Just like knowing you're thinking about convincing one of the guys to drive you into town so you can run away from the island is my business."

I glare at him. So what if I was thinking exactly that? "Todd. You're being really sweet, but after a few weeks you'd be bored with me and by then I'd have my heart all torn up and I... I'd rather not."

Todd stops in front of me, so I have to crane my neck to look up at him. Without warning, he bends down, bracing his arms on either side of me, and stares into my eyes. "So you do think I'm too old for you?" His tone is even, but his gaze is anything but. It's hot and simmering, anticipatory.

I shake my head quickly, my curls flying. "No! Of course not."

His lips claim mine. Even more possessively than last time, which I wouldn't have thought possible. His lips never leave my mouth as he sinks to his knees by the side of the bed, pushing me back until I'm lying flat against the silky sheets. His tongue plunders my mouth, his hands heavy on my hips. My fingers lace through his thick hair, holding him close. With a groan, he finally pulls back, then darts in to nip at my lower lip just enough to make me gasp and reach for him again.

"So it's not the age gap, it's not a question of attraction, and it's not about hating the music." I open my mouth to correct him, but he places a finger over my lips. "I don't care, Lilah, so you shouldn't either. But baby, that only leaves one thing I can think of that you could be hung up on. Money. Am I right?"

I hate how shallow that makes me sound, but reluctantly I nod. "That's what I said already."

"There's an easy fix for that. We get married and then you automatically have half of what I have. Sell one cup of coffee on top of that and you'll be wealthier than I am." He yawns lightly as if he didn't just verbally hand over millions of dollars.

"Todd! I'm not marrying you without a prenup. Don't be crazy."

He grins and rocks back on his heels. "Good, we're making progress. You're now at least entertaining the idea of a wedding. And baby," he sobers, "there will not be any kind of prenup. You are stuck with me. At least for my few remaining years. The good news is since I'll be so busy chasing nurses at the assisted living center where you've stashed me, I won't get in your hair too much."

I push his shoulders in aggravation, and he sits back on his ass, still grinning at me. "Relax, Lilah. I'm good for at least another fifty or sixty years, according to my doctor. Who, by the way, is happy to take as much of my money as he can get his hands on. You can come with me next time and watch how he does it."

"Ass." It comes out more fondly than I would have expected.

He winks and I find it charming, which means I'm in trouble because generally I find winking to be cheesy and pointless. But when Todd does it, I go a little gooey in the middle.

I bite my lip as I watch his face, so full of life and energy. I think I love him; I realize. It's not just a little crush on a handsome older man. I cast my gaze down, avoiding the sudden intensity of emotions, and the bed I'm sitting on catches my attention once again. "Hey, how come you have a bed in your closet? It's not like you're short of bedrooms."

Todd sobers instantly and looks a little hesitant. "I'll tell you all about it tomorrow, okay? It's nothing horrible and well, I guess you could say it's to do with shadows from ancient history. I want you to know. Hell, you deserve to know, but not right now. Today is about convincing you not to run away, not for giving you ammunition to head for the hills." His smile is wry and I reach my hand out to lay it on his shoulder. I need to be touching him, and my heart melts a little further when he leans his cheek down to rest on my fingers.

TODD

I almost don't recognize this feeling of possibilities and excitement about the future. It's been that long. Longer still since I even imagined I was in love and I never really believed it even then. Just seemed like what everyone else was doing and, well... fake it till you make it. I might have made it in terms of fame and fortune, but romantic relationships? Not even close. Not until I happened to be on the receiving end of Lilah's smile, which turned out to be aimed at the person behind me in line, but never mind. I felt it radiate over me and decided right then and there I wanted it aimed directly at me.

Reluctantly, I pull away from her. She needs to get dressed so we can eat and I can take her to the clinic and I'd be pushing my luck to suggest I stay and watch. Still... "You need any help?"

She's on to me based on the way her eyes narrow. "No, I've been dressing myself for a couple of decades now — think I've got the hang of it."

"Worth a shot," I say as I stand and lean down to give her one last kiss. "Get dressed then, but stay here. I'll be back to get you once I've brought the car around to the front."

"I thought we were going to eat first?" She's frowning like I've suggested she needed to go on a diet. I wouldn't dare and she doesn't anyhow. If anything, she's gotten too thin. I don't know if she's been trying to save money by cutting back on food or if it's all stress related to the situation. But either way, she's not leaving the house until I see her eat a decent meal.

"We're not going anywhere until you eat, baby. Don't fret. Just thinking ahead. The clinic doesn't open until nine, anyway."

She's rolling her eyes now. Good.

The entrance to the closet is a sliding pocket door, so as I step out I bring to almost closed just in case someone wanders in here while I'm outside. And I shut the main door to the bedroom firmly, anyway. The guys are decent but frequently clueless. I'd rather avert a crisis by shutting a few doors.

Like the boat, I have way too much horsepower for the island in the six-bay garage. No, nobody needs that many vehicles unless they're a collector, which I'm not. Nor is my Uncle Lou the original intended owner. The architect knew insecure new money when he saw it, and twenty years ago I was brimming with the stuff. God, this house is such a waste.

In the end, I settle for the ugliest and most basic of the lot. Not because Lilah doesn't deserve to arrive in style in the vintage Jaguar (which probably isn't in any better shape than her car at the bottom of the hill). But because the old truck is a good height for her to get in and out of with a busted ankle. Basically, I can lift her up and down from the bench seat easily and there's plenty of leg room. It's the one I end up driving most often, honestly, when I bother to drive at all. It's a bit of a walk into town from here, but still doable — unless you've landed wrong in that damn pothole, of course.

When I head back into the house, the guys are jabbering in the kitchen over the faint sizzle of bacon. Which must mean the pancakes haven't started yet. Still, I'd better get Lilah down here before they eat it all. Taking the stairs two at a time, I'm a tiny bit relieved that I'm not panting when I arrive at the curved landing. But that satisfaction fades fast when I open the closet door and find Lilah sitting where I left her, tears streaming down her face.

"Lilah? What the hell happened? I was only gone for two minutes. Are you hurt? Did you try to walk?"

She shakes her head frantically while the tears trail down her splotchy cheeks. Worst of all, she's stiff in my arms when I sit down next to her and try to soothe her.

That's when I hear them, clear as a bell, the voices of the guys and the clinking of silverware through the heating vent in the closet. I've lived here for years and never noticed that, but then it's not like when other people are in the house I'm hanging out in here. Not when they're talking in the kitchen, at any rate.

Roman says something about growing bell peppers on his patio. I doubt that would get this kind of reaction from Lilah. Not unless she had a truly traumatic food incident in childhood, but even then…

"Was it something the guys said?" I ask her as gently as I can. She just stares at me and hiccups. "Right. I'll take that as a yes. Be right back."

In the kitchen, Roman is gathering silverware while Lance starts ladling batter into fancy swirls on the grill.

"What the fuck did you guys say to upset Lilah?" I growl.

Everyone pauses and looks up, surprised. "Lilah's not here, man. Besides, we've just been shooting the regular shit. No need to pick on your girl." Karl stares at me like I've grown two heads and lost my sanity in the process.

"Someone must have said something big. I've never seen her cry like that. What were you talking about before Roman started in on growing peppers?" I'm beyond exasperated.

"Uh… well, Lance was filling us in on the growth on his ass. Which I'd rather not have known about, although it's good he got it checked, I guess. And… before that… oh. Ernie did say something about your crush on Ms. Ringstadt. What did you say, Ernie? That was funny."

Ernest pops in from the conservatory off the dining room. "Hmmm? Oh, I was just remembering how you used to mope around when she announced she was getting married. Remember, TK? You vowed to never marry because of it."

Now I really am growling, thinking how Lilah must have heard this. I shout over the flying banter, "Did any of you think to mention that I was only eight at the time?"

"Uh, no? We were too. So what?" Karl looks perplexed, but he's not the one I need to explain things to. I rush back up the stairs again. I'm definitely getting my cardio in for the day.

Lilah is not where I left her. I panic until I hear water running in the bathroom, but even then I'm worried she tried to walk, so I barge right in. She screams lightly. Because of her previous crying jag, it comes out as more of a croak, but I still feel bad for scaring her on top of the guys' stupidity.

"Are you okay?" I notice she's keeping her bad leg bent, so probably she hopped in here.

She nods stiffly and I sag against the door frame. "You didn't hear their explanation a few minutes ago, did you?"

"There's more?" She doesn't sound anywhere near thrilled.

I scoop her up and carry her over to the normal-size bed. She's still stiff and bristly in my arms. "Let me recap just in case I missed anything. The guys don't know their own level of stupid sometimes. You heard something about my unrequited love for my math teacher, but they made it sound like some more recent grand passion that I've never recovered from. Right?"

Lilah blinks slowly and then gapes at me. "Math teacher? How old were you?"

I nod firmly. "Eight. Ms. Ringstadt smelled good, which is about all it took for me in those days. Then she went and married the history teacher from the high school. I saw her a few years later, and she'd gotten fat and smelled like cabbage. So clearly my heart had moved on. By eleven I was convinced girls were useless and then there was the unobtainable Misty from your favorite song. She didn't give any of us the time of day and, quite frankly, we were all secretly happy about that. She was scary."

Lilah is finally giggling a little at this recital. Then she heaves a huge sigh. "But that means you've always had a thing for older women."

"That's what you got out of that? Did you consider that I explored that direction and found it wanting before you were even born?"

"I'll take it under advisement but I'm not convinced," she says primly but I can see the hints of a smile peaking through the clouds.

"Food will help with that. Come on, I'm starving." I pick her up again, and this time she tucks her head against my shoulder. And when I set her down at the table, she looks around at the guys who are staring at her nervously and says, "Tell me more about this sexy math teacher. I need the lowdown on my competition."

They look at each other in shock and then howl with laughter. Good thing I claimed her first.

She charms them. There's no two ways about it. By the end of breakfast, I'm back to growling at everyone. She's mine. Of course, they're going to worship the ground she walks on, who wouldn't? But they can damn well keep a respectful thirty-foot distance while they do it.

Lilah and a few of the guys keep giving me odd looks. I'm pretty sure I know why, but I'm not in the mood to address it. Maybe if we can just get this damn album done, they'll clear out and I can have her to myself. I've got plans.

6

LILAH

I'm still in a state of shock, really. A megazillionaire rock star is worried about me. Genuinely concerned. It helps if I forget the fame stuff and just focus on Todd.

Todd is worried about my feelings, and my ankle, and the state of my business. Todd spends a lot of time worrying, I'm coming to realize. No wonder he's grumpy with the world. And even that is a lot to take in.

Because back when I thought he was just rich and minor league famous, I didn't really see what he would find enticing about me. Does he actually feel the same delicious thrill of possibility when he's holding me? I need to ask him. Sometime when there isn't an audience of overgrown teenagers listening to every word and I'm feeling very brave. Definitely not now. Not when there's an entire waiting room of local islanders all sneaking peeks at us over the tops of the three-year-old family magazines. The crinkled assortment that counts as reading material in the waiting room of the one and only medical clinic.

Todd is still pouting because they brought a wheelchair over for me and he's not allowed to carry me inside the clinic. He's making up for it by playing with my fingers while we wait, which is distracting me from almost everything else.

When my name is called, he assumes he's coming back with me, which is really very sweet. And since this visit was entirely his idea, I'd rather he hear the verdict that I'm completely fine from the nurse practitioner herself.

It turns out I am mostly okay, but ordered to use crutches for at least two to three days. Now we're both unhappy. Me because walking and normal life are on hold and Todd because his mission to carry me everywhere has once again been thwarted.

He perks up when he realizes I won't be able to manage the stairs to my apartment. "She's staying with me," he says flatly when the nurse asks if I have someone to help me. I roll my eyes but nod. I don't have any other practical options. Not unless I want to sleep on the floor of the cafe and that definitely wouldn't be good for business. Might violate a few health ordinances too, not that the island worries too much about that kind of thing.

Naturally, Todd has the bill all paid by the time I awkwardly make my way back to the front on my new crutches. He holds the door for me patiently but breathes a sigh of relief when he lifts me up into the truck and tucks the crutches in the gap behind the seats. "Those need to stay on ground level. I'm already having nightmares about you breaking your neck while attempting to navigate the stairs."

"Maybe I should stay downstairs too? You have a guestroom down there. Why can't I stay in that room?"

"Because I want you with me? Because the guys sometimes forget where they are and wander around naked?"

"They do?" I'm fascinated.

"No! But why do you sound so interested?" Todd sounds so put out I can't hold back the giggles.

"I don't know how rock stars behave in their natural environment. This is sort of like a nature show on TV."

He growls, "You better not be remotely interested in the mating habits of anyone that isn't me."

"Hmmm. Maybe I'd better do some comparative research so I..."

Todd grabs my hand and gives a sharp nip to the fleshy part of my thumb. "Behave. But I'm glad you're feeling well enough to be teasing." He slants a smile in my direction that warms my insides. In no time he parks behind the cafe and turns off the engine. "Give me your keys, love, and I'll go grab your things. Anything in particular you want?"

I hesitate. "Can't you take me up there?"

"I could. But then it will be several trips back down for you and your stuff. We can always come back and get more."

Fine. I've put him out enough and I don't want to strain his back any more than necessary. "Just some basics, I guess. Loose pants that will fit over my ankle, some pajamas." He frowns at that, but nods and gets out of the truck. "Be back in a jiffy. I'll call if I have questions."

"To what? My phone is lying somewhere on that road, remember?"

"Oh. Right. Well, I'll do my best. Do you want my phone while you wait? You can stalk all my apps and photos."

I should say no, right? But an excited little tingle has me holding out my hand with a grin. He unlocks it and hands it over with a wink. Then he gives me a brief salute before heading into the building. I sit there in the truck facing down the alley and try to remember exactly how messy I left the place before heading out to make my apology. That seems like a week ago at least, rather than yesterday. Then I quickly dive into his phone before it relocks. Because I'm damn curious about what makes Todd tick.

First off, he has old man apps on his phone. Things like the weather and news channels. He has one reading app and I eagerly click into that to see what he reads. Thrillers. And some non-fiction about architecture and house design. There are no games and no dating apps. I flip into his photos, hoping for some revealing insights.

Family is important to him. There are pictures of the guys and his uncle and an older woman I assume is his mom standing next to a man of similar age who doesn't look at all like Todd. Step-dad maybe? I'm surprised to find that there are one or two of me. Not stalkery, just casual ones from the coffee shop. I vaguely remember posing for one, but didn't think too much about it at the time. I think I thought he was a tourist collecting local color to show off when he got back to the big city.

Todd comes out of the building carrying two stuffed duffel bags that he tosses into the back of the truck, then opens my door to hand me a smaller tote bag. "I grabbed your laptop and a few other things I thought you might like."

"Thanks." I peer into the bag. He remembered to find the charger and also a few notebooks and the paperback I was reading. He wasn't to know I've read it five million times and can practically recite it. I close the bag and watch as the neighborhood disappears behind us. "Do you think there's a chance my phone is still alive?" I ask quietly.

He spares me a sympathetic glance. "Maybe. Doubtful. Why don't you start calling it when we get near the pothole of doom and I'll go extra slow? Maybe we'll hear it."

I nod, happy with that plan because at least it's something to try since I can't exactly go sifting through the bushes. My heart sinks when my number immediately goes to voicemail. "It's dead."

"Sorry, baby. We'll order you a new one as soon as we get in."

"No. You've done more than enough for me. I'll shop around and find a used one."

He growls in frustration. "It's just money, Lilah. Why can't I spend it the way I want to?"

I raise my eyebrows at him in shock. "Because I'm not your responsibility, and I don't ever want you to think I want you for your money. I don't." I finish quietly. I'm sad that I can't find the words to get this across to him.

He rolls his eyes at me. "Lilah, I get it, I do. But I'm still ordering six phones and they can either sit in the drawer or you can pick one to use."

"Six! Where did that come from?"

"Because I can see that I'm going to have to be overly extravagant to get you to take anything, so it won't all be wasted." He nods with satisfaction. "Buy one, you'll refuse it. Buy six, you might consider using one. Buy twelve and you might actually take one out of the house with you."

"Twelve? Are you escalating?"

"Getting smart in my old age."

"Wasting money is not smart."

"Then take the damn phone."

I huff with frustration because, really. "Fine," I grumble and poke him in the side when he can't hold back the satisfied smirk.

This won't last for long. I guess the least I can do is try to wring the most happiness I can out of the time I have with him.

TODD

I can tell Lilah is worn out from the clinic visit and her first few forays on crutches. So naturally, I'm hovering as she awkwardly makes her way from the truck to the front door of the house. I parked as close as I could manage, but it's still a few hundred feet. She's so busy glaring at me that she almost puts her crutches into the dip between paving slabs and I have to catch her before she goes down.

"Watch where you're going, baby, or I'm going to confiscate those things," I warn her.

"Then I'll hop," she sasses back.

My grunt is the most diplomatic reaction I can manage as I open the door and keep my eagle eyes on her as she navigates getting over the doorjamb. I'm literally having to lock my muscles to resist sweeping her up and carrying her. The fact that she sighs with relief when she's safely in the entryway tells me she's more nervous about this than she's letting on. Makes my next move easier. "Lilah, if I catch you even near the stairs with those things, you'll regret it."

Her glare is adorable. "People manage stairs with crutches all the time."

"People aren't you. Do it for me, I'm old. You don't want me to have a heart attack." I'm not above playing the sympathy card if it means she stays in one piece.

She just humphs. I realize I'm half-waiting for her to tell me I'm not old. Lilah figures that out too, which is why her eyes are twinkling and her lips are pursed, holding back a grin.

"Brat. Come on, I'm going to get you settled in the living room and then the guys and I will get out of your hair so you can rest."

"Where are you going?" She's curiously eyeing the front door I shut behind us.

I shake my head. "Downstairs. I've got a sound

proof studio and offices down there. We need to get some practice in before we get to the recording sessions."

She nods and slowly makes her way into the living room. She lets me help her maneuver down onto the couch, thankfully. I'm tempted to set the crutches over against the wall where she can't get to them. But I know that wouldn't really stop her, so I set them against the arm of the couch instead. I round up a throw blanket from the chest in the corner. It still has its tags on it. Can't even remember where it came from, but word to the wise — guys aren't really that into throws. I'm past needing to look tough by shivering to death when it's cold, but in those cases a full-size blanket is called for, not this miniature crap. But it is very soft and fluffy and tucks around Lilah's smaller frame with room to spare. She sighs and pushes her hands under one of the throw pillows on the couch.

"Baby? Don't go to sleep just yet."

"Hmm?" she raises her head with curiosity. I bring a cordless phone over to her and show her the intercom function. "Just press three and it will sound inside the studio. Don't hesitate if you need to get up. We're just going to be messing around. Nothing that can't be interrupted."

"'S'okay. Three. Got it." Her eyes close and I hesitate. Somehow I'm not trusting that I can leave her alone here. I double-check that the door is locked and watch her breathing, noting the moment when she shifts into true sleep. Right. That's what she needs, not me creeping on her like an overprotective bear.

I round up the guys from around the house, warning them to keep it down until we're in the basement. To a man, they roll their eyes at me. "Jesus, TK, she got you by the balls or what?" That's from Lance, naturally, who has certainly fucked his way through a good portion of the female population but to my knowledge has never been in love.

I narrow my eyes at him. "Someday, you idiot, you'll know what it feels like."

For a brief second there's a flash of pain in his eyes, but then it's gone and he's flinging his hands in the air. Since we don't really do that deep emotional shit, we all turn our attention to work. Well, sort of. These reunions always require a day or so of pure messing around like we're kids again planning our big future in someone's garage, back when we didn't know any better.

Roman starts picking out the chords to a popular sappy love song and then Ernie, the traitor, starts ad-libbing lyrics that imply my manhood is now firmly in a woman's possession. Can't really deny it and my lips are twitching as I stand there, arms folded, letting them get it out of their systems.

"Maybe stick to your day job, Ernie? Leave the

vocals to me?" I interject when he pauses to launch into his improvised chorus. I grin when he flips me the bird while moaning about giving up all the other women in the world. He makes it sound like a bad thing.

A couple of hours later and we've progressed to more 'real' music, but it's still just playing around, when suddenly the guys go silent, the twang of instruments dying abruptly. I swivel to find out what the fuck they're staring at. Lilah's leaning against the outer door frame, a soft smile on her face. Instantly I'm on my feet and opening the door. "Lilah, you okay?"

She nods, not losing the smile. "I thought you guys would be all serious and marking out chords and stuff."

"Naw, that part comes later," Roman chimes in from the side.

Lilah's gaze swings from him back to me. "Todd, what's the matter?"

"What did I tell you about using the crutches on stairs?" I fold my arms over my chest to keep from shaking her. Images of her tumbling down the basement steps making my heart race. They're carpeted, but that wouldn't stop her from breaking her neck.

"Oh, I just doubled them up on my right and hung onto the railing. Perfectly safe." She waves a dismissive hand until my growl startles her into silence.

"Not okay, Lilah." I pull the chair I'd been straddling into the corner of the room and then pick her up, crutches and all. Depositing her in the chair, I reach up to the shelf behind her head and grab a pair of hearing-protection headphones. "You stay right here where I can keep an eye on you. I'll let you know what your punishment for the stairs is later." I release the headphones onto her ears while she rolls her eyes.

When I turn back to the guys, they're staring at me in shock. Then the smothered laughter starts while my glare intensifies. "Get back to work," I finally grumble, but it's a long minute before Roman heaves a sigh and launches into one of his new tunes, a little angry but with an underlying happy beat. Suits my mood to a T. Now I've got to come up with something that will convince Lilah not to take any more risks with her sweet body.

7

LILAH

Never in a million years did I think I'd be sitting in the same room while Unspeakable Noise goofs around with pop songs. I don't have to be a fan of their music to be impressed by what I'm witnessing. These guys are world-class musicians and it shows.

I'm also a little shocked at the way Todd yelled at me. So I'm sure my eyes are probably hanging out of my head and that's why one of the guys makes eye contact when Todd's back is turned and winks.

I flush slightly but relax just a tiny bit. So this dramatic bent isn't completely normal for him, although nobody seems surprised by his grumpiness. More worry, I guess, and maybe that means he really does care about me? More than just as a friend or a fling or a lost soul that needs protecting because he truly is a genuinely nice guy. It's the inherent hero complex idea that really worries me because that would explain all the sweet things he said to me earlier.

The earphones he plunked on my head are good ones, so while I can just barely make out a bit of the bass, I can't hear the guys' voices at all. I'm tempted to pull them off so I can listen, but that would probably enrage the beast. So instead I use it as an opportunity to study body language — Todd's, of course. He's magnetic when he's in performance mode and since he gave me his chair, he's pacing back and forth in the small room like a caged panther. Now and then, his eyes flick to me, probably to make sure I haven't escaped.

After about twenty minutes, I notice his gaze sharpen when it lands on me. There's renewed heat in the way he regards me, like he thought of something else to get angry about or had some kind of intriguing inspiration. For all I know, it's both.

Watching the band, even though I can see they're playing around from their perspective, their professionalism is obvious. And that makes me doubt once again what Todd sees in me. It's like a renowned food critic taking up with a woman who gets excited when the three-dollar wine goes on sale. I can't discuss any of the stuff they're doing or have done. Well, aside from my unfortunate blathering that created this whole mess to begin with.

Maybe I should just sneak out and head back upstairs. It's probably past time to start contacting the real-estate agents on the bigger islands, see if they're willing to even take a listing for the coffee shop. That's something I can do now if I use Todd's landline in the kitchen. That way, maybe I'll have some appointments ready when I can move around easily again. I sigh and start to push myself out of the chair. I reach down for my crutches before I get too vertical to grab them, only to find them moving away under their own power. I look up and there's Todd, glowering. I pull the headphones off with my free hand and wince when they clap against my head. Word of warning, always use two hands to remove serious hearing protection. Those suckers hurt!

"Where do you think you're going?" He's practically shouting, and the noise after so much silence is jarring.

"You're busy and I've got things to do. Since you won't even let me listen..."

Todd growls and my belly flips. He's seriously sexy when he's angry. That makes me giggle, reminding me of that demeaning phrase in old movies about a woman being pretty when she's mad. Of course Todd has no idea why I'm laughing, so I shouldn't be surprised when he picks me up like I weigh nothing and tosses me over his shoulder. He turns around to grumble at the other guys, "Go away. Lilah and I need to have a serious talk."

I can't see them, of course, but I can practically hear them exchanging amused glances. One of them, I'm not sure which, calls out, "Lilah? You okay with that? He's not usually this stupid."

I eye the curve of Todd's perfect ass. "I'm good. Maybe check that I'm still alive in a few hours?" I answer breathlessly. Partly from being upside down, but also the way Todd's hand is gripping my thigh. It's not a polite hold, it's possessive and firm and I really rather like it.

There are a few chuckles and one of them bends to wave fingers where I can see them as they head out of the room. When the tromp of feet going up the stairs dies down, Todd moves us out into the hallway as well. "Time to teach you a much-needed lesson, Lilah," he says grimly as he carries me down the hall in the opposite direction from the stairs.

I gulp when Todd flips me back right side up, still holding me close until I get a firm footing on my good leg. He didn't bring the crutches with us. I'm not sure if that's because he intends to keep me prisoner or if it was just impractical to carry them as well as me. I'm nervously watching him until I notice the slight twinkle in his eyes and relax a little. Maybe I shouldn't though.

My nervous anticipation rebuilds when I realize we're stopped in front of a locked door in the basement. It's a finished basement, with the same bleached pine floorboards as upstairs, so it's hardly a dungeon. Still, I'm not sure anyone else knows about this room or if they can hear anything from upstairs…

Which I discover may be part of Todd's thinking when he unlocks the door with a code that he doesn't even try to hide from me, although even now I can't remember it.

Inside, the room is surprisingly corporate. It's an office, there's no two ways about it, with file cabinets and the works. I don't really think of rock stars having file cabinets or anything practical, really. But clearly Todd isn't typical, and he's the first rock star I've ever met, so probably best if you go and do your own survey on that one if you're interested.

There's a huge heavy wood desk and a very elegant leather office chair with a high back but no other chairs in the room. I balance on my one leg uncertainly near the desk where he deposited me while Todd opens and shuts cabinets, pulling out supplies. He places a legal-size yellow pad on the desk and three pens. He walks out of the room briefly and returns with a full glass of water, which he sets neatly to the right of the pens. He shuts the door firmly and then sits down in the chair with his legs spread. Oh dear God, he's not planning on spanking me, is he? I'm not sure how I feel about that. Surely it's my business if I want to take a risk going down a few stairs safely. I was hanging on to the railing.

Todd's worried eyes sweep over me. "I need to know that you really understand how much you scared me, baby. So show me you're willing to learn a new lesson and prove to me you truly get it so I can relax."

Oh fuck. I stare at him, wondering briefly if he's just trying to manipulate me, but all I see is genuine concern and outright fear. If this will make him feel better… Reluctantly, I nod.

He grabs my hand and tugs me towards him, making me hop briefly before pulling me down on his lap. Not over it. So that's something. "Todd?" I manage to get out. My fresh confusion is obvious in my voice.

"Worried, were you?" He's laughing at me gently. "You may be wishing I was going to spank you after about ten minutes of what I have planned. This, my lovely Lilah, is both old-fashioned school-girl punishment combined with some new-age California therapy. Plus a little extra of my own personal touch because you are most definitely not a little girl and I think I deserve a little something after what you've put me through."

I blink. That didn't explain much.

"You're about to write sentences, baby. Over and over and over. You'll write them while I touch you and while you suck my fingers. If you make a mistake, you'll have to start the page over, so take your time. When you've *neatly* filled a page, you're going to read each line aloud."

Fuck. He's right. A spanking would be over much, much sooner. But my pussy likes the idea of all the touching. I can already feel myself clenching in anticipation.

"How many sentences are we talking? A hundred?"

He shakes his head. "That's for kids, sweetness. I think there are about fifty lines on each page. I'm going to give you ten sentences and you'll write a full page of each — without any mistakes — so I suggest you take your time. Ready?"

I shake my head no, but he grins and turns me around on his lap so I'm sitting there with my legs spread wide over his, facing the desk. He pulls the pad closer and hands me a pen.

"Now, I'm going to dictate the first sentence and you'll write it at the top of the page."

I sigh, but hold the pen ready.

"At forty-six…" he starts and I dutifully write the numerals, but he stops me with, "Nope, spell it out, Lilah."

I sigh and cross out the numerals and then write them out longhand. "At forty-six, Todd is the perfect age to fuck me senseless…" I snort and Todd pinches my thigh. "At this rate, I'm going to have to order dinner down here. Pay attention. Now, where was I?… Todd is the perfect age to fuck me senseless and I can't wait to be stretched by his massive cock."

I write it out, trying to hold back the giggles and not succeeding very well. Todd leans in over my shoulder. "There's a comma after forty-six and you can end the sentence with either a period or an exclamation point. Your choice."

I roll my eyes and firmly press in a simple period. I'm not feeding his ego with an exclamation point, even if it is more accurate. I still have all my doubts from before, but I'm curious to see where he's planning on taking this, so I guess the deep conversation can wait until later.

"Good. Now you're going to suck on my fingers while you copy that down the page." Suddenly my mouth is full of Todd. Even his fingers taste delicious, but I'm confused as to what this has to do with anything. I look back at him as best I can with a question in my eyes, but he just smiles. "I'll explain it *after* you're done. Get writing, sweetness."

I turn back and start carefully copying the words. Ten lines in, I fuck up because Todd's other hand has started roaming on my thigh. That hand comes off my body to rip the paper off the pad. "Start again, Lilah," he sighs with mock disappointment. He's enjoying this… way too much.

It takes forever to fill the page. Between his fingers in my mouth and the ones teasing me lower down, I have shit concentration. I have to suck his fingers so I can swallow and not drool down my front. And that means I have to focus on one letter at a time. When

I place the last period on the last sentence, Todd removes his fingers from my mouth. But they join his other hand between my thighs and start making slow circles over my pussy through my pants, which are already soaking wet.

His right hand leaves me again and grabs a pen. "Now start reading them aloud. I'm going to mark off each one so you don't try to cheat."

I groan. The reading is a little easier than the writing but not much. I'm more than a little distracted by the hard length swelling against my ass. Seems Todd isn't as unaffected by this as he pretends. Maybe it's hearing the words from me? I file that away for the future and make my voice as throaty as I can manage, lingering on the words 'stretch' and 'cock'. Todd's free hand clenches down hard on my left thigh.

TODD

My bright idea has backfired badly and my pulsing cock is proof that I've lost control of the situation. Lilah is learning a completely different lesson than the one I intended to teach. But the way she's wriggling on my lap with occasional breathless giggles is so fucking entrancing I don't even care.

I groan when she finishes reciting the second set of sentences. *I am a beautiful, intelligent woman who is willing to accept Todd's help since I already hold his heart.* She struggled with that one. I could feel her internal conflict stiffening her spine. But by the end her voice held more confidence, and she was starting to tease me again. Now she's looking at me like I should give her another sentence, but I don't think I can last without cumming in my pants.

"New rule," I groan, "two sentences a day for five days."

Her eyes go round with shock. "But… work. The coffee shop? You have the guys…"

I shake my head violently, unable to form words with the way her round ass is bouncing against me. "Mine." I gather her close and stand up, intent on carrying her back to my lair.

Lilah seems oblivious to my reversion to caveman. She just keeps talking. "What are you doing? What about my crutches? I can manage. Todd?"

Finally, I set her down gently on the bed in the master bedroom. Ostensibly my room, but it never felt like it until Lilah got here. Now it's all I can do not to pounce on her. "Need a minute," I choke out and stumble out of the room intent on getting outside and sticking my cock in a snowdrift until my raging hard-on can return some of the blood to my brain. Too bad we're months away from actual snow, so

I have to be content with standing in the driveway letting the icy rain pour over me.

That's where Karl finds me. Only he comes armed with an umbrella. "We drew straws. I lost. What the fuck is wrong with you, TK?"

I spare him a brief glance before scrubbing the rain off my face with my hands. "Trying to be a gentleman. It's killing me."

He snorts. "Then why are you doing it? She seems pretty into you."

I glare at him. "Because I'm going to marry her and she deserves respect."

"So fuck her with respect. I hear that's possible." He sounds doubtful.

"I thought I made it clear you guys aren't even supposed to think about her," I growl.

He holds up both his hands like he's worried about my sanity. "I'm not, dude. Get a grip. Maybe talk to Lilah about this instead of standing out here in the rain? She's probably worried about you."

That gets through to me and I follow him back inside.

8

LILAH

Todd finally comes back in the room, soaking wet and looking… pissed? Frustrated? I'm not sure how to read his expression. I reach out and snag his hand, pulling him down to sit next to me on the bed. I don't care if everything gets wet in the process.

"What's wrong?" I can be blunt when I need to be.

He rakes his free hand over his face, sending water droplets flying. "Nothing, baby. You want anything to eat?" His eyes are slightly feral, like his control is at a snapping point.

"Stop trying to change the subject. What's going on?"

"Nothing you need to worry about."

"Well, I am worried. You… do whatever that was in the basement and then just drop me here — frustrated, I might add — and disappear. Then you come back, wet and angry. Spill." I try to express in my voice that I'm not mad, but I will insist on an answer.

He eyes me warily. "What happened to the other Lilah? The one that gets sweetly flustered and embarrassed?"

"She was left high and dry without an orgasm. That's what."

His lips curve into a smirk. "Ah, baby. I can take care of that for you."

I bat his reaching hand away. "Later. Maybe. Explanation now."

His hand keeps coming though, palming my breast before he leans down for a deep kiss. He smells of rain and impending thunder.

"Fine, but you don't get to escape your punishment for the rest of the week," he concedes with a stern twist to his lips.

I give him some serious side-eye. He sighs heavily. "The point of that exercise is to engage all five senses while entrenching new beliefs. Usually it doesn't involve sexy stuff, but there's no denying arousal goes straight to the most primal part of the brain, which is supposed to have a more profound impact."

I think that over. It sort of makes sense, but not entirely. "Okaaay, but then why leave me when it was clear you were, um… ready for something more?"

Todd's lips curve down, and his fingers tangle with mine. "You still don't quite believe I'm serious about you. That this isn't something convenient or temporary. I'm not going to fuck you until you understand that this is permanent. T'il death do us part, follow you to the ends of the earth permanent."

I gape at him. I mean, I heard some similar words earlier, but he's right. I didn't realize how serious he was. "Umm."

His smile is a little wry. "Exactly. We'll get there, but I'm not losing ground while you believe I'm just using you to get my rocks off. Now you, on the other hand, you have a problem I can fix right now."

Todd dips his head again, but I push back on his shoulders. "That still doesn't explain why you're all wet."

"Just needed to cool off."

"And whatever you're planning on right now isn't going to send you out there again?" I'm doubtful and he's really wet.

He grimaces. "Maybe. But I can deal with that. You're worth it, Lilah. You always have been," he says that so calmly and quietly it takes a minute to sink in and then tears are coursing down my cheeks. Todd pulls me close against his chest and I laugh through the tears because he's so wet all the water just melds together.

I try to hug him in return, but my arms are pinned so I have to settle for nestling in as close as I can manage. He runs his fingers through my hair. "Sure you don't want me to make you feel better?"

I chuckle through my remaining tears. "I'd feel guilty if you won't accept the same. But I do feel better just being next to you. I think that's why I can't let myself believe you want something serious. It's too scary to think of losing that."

"You won't."

We sit there for I don't know how long, but eventually my stomach rumbles and Todd jerks to attention. "Fuck, you need dinner."

I nod. "I can go downstairs, you know."

He narrows his eyes at me. "Not on your life. I'll bring something up." He checks his watch. "Sorry, baby. It's late, probably bed after that, yeah?"

I roll my eyes. "If I'm not getting hot rock star sex, then I guess so."

Todd grins in response, his perfect teeth flashing, and the way his eyes sparkle in appreciation has me reaching for him, ready to change his mind. But he moves out of the way and off the bed. "Stop tempting me, sexy coffee shop girl. Be back in a minute." He leans down to drop a smacking kiss on my lips and then strides from the room.

I'm yawning by the time he comes back with a plate of pizza and a mug of tea.

"Interesting combination," I remark as he sets the tray down.

"Didn't think you should have wine yet while you're still on pain meds and there wasn't much else. I can get you some water?"

"It's fine. Sit?" I pat the bed next to me, but he shakes his head.

"You're too tempting, baby. I'm going to lock up and then get ready for bed. I'll be back to in a minute to carry you to the bathroom. Don't you dare try to hop."

I roll my eyes at him while stuffing my mouth with pizza. It's my favorite combination of fresh vegies and extra cheese.

"I mean it, Lilah. I've never spanked a woman in my life but if it will keep you from injuring yourself..." He leaves the threat hanging in midair and I'm still in mid-chew as I hear his feet going down the stairs. I don't know if I'd mind being spanked by Todd now that he's brought it up more than once. I wonder if he secretly wants to do that to me? I try to imagine his hand connecting with my ass, but I still can't picture it. I grimace and finish my pizza. Just as I'm setting the tray aside, Todd comes back and gives me a warning look.

"Just give me your arm, then. It's like twenty feet away, I think I can make it."

"What if I want to carry you?" he mutters.

"You'll live," I respond dryly, not reminding him that the nurse said I could try putting a little weight on it with the crutches tomorrow. That's going to be fun with Todd hovering like a nervous hen.

TODD

I use the excuse of needing to kill the overhead lights to tuck Lilah into bed. Really, it's because I want any chance to touch her. And now that she's not hurting quite so badly, the frown line between her brows has smoothed out. But when she tucks her hand under her cheek and closes her eyes, my heart twinges because she looks so damn young.

"Why are you staring at me?" she inquires softly, without opening her eyes.

Startled, I move to switch off the lights. "Sorry, just being a dirty old man. Night, Lilah."

She snorts and shifts in the bed. "The way you talk, anyone would think you were a hundred years old. If anything, I'm way too old to be your trophy girlfriend. Not to mention too fat."

I growl, "You're perfect, and don't you forget it. I can work that into your sentences tomorrow."

"Maybe get your arguments straight first. If I'm perfect, then I'm not too young, right?"

"Going to bed now." Of course she's right. I'm having some kind of problem being happy, I guess. I head into the closet and the bed that now doesn't seem like quite as much of a refuge as it used to be.

"Todd?" Lilah calls, sounding confused.

"Yeah?" I turn back.

"Where are you going? You're not sleeping in the bed? But you locked the door."

"I'll sleep in the closet. Won't be the first time."

There's a long pregnant pause, the dark taking on a thick texture in the room.

"Because you've had gimpy women taking up your bed?" she asks slowly.

"No. You're the first woman to be there, gimpy or otherwise. Some other time, angel." I don't really want her seeing that part of me, not until she's sure about the rest of it. Then maybe, just maybe, she'll agree the pros outweigh the cons. Unless she's blinded by love, I doubt very much she'd come to that conclusion.

I ache with tension when I stretch out on the narrow bed, beneath the short row of dress shirts

I never wear. I listen for Lilah in the next room, but hear nothing.

My mind won't shut down and eventually I try to string lyrics together as a way to occupy it — if I'm lucky, it's enough to put me to sleep when nothing seems to work. Not tonight. My thoughts are full of Lilah, smiling in warm greeting in the coffee shop, crying in my arms, thinking she's been mean when she really hadn't, except maybe to herself.

Before long I'm sitting up, reaching for the small overhead light, barely remembering to shut the closet door so I don't wake Lilah. I keep a small notebook and pen in here for just this reason. But checking the date of the last entry it's been a few years since I bothered. I force myself not to censor the words, just write down what's flowing through my brain. I'll look at it more critically in the morning. Now is just for letting the muse flow. And she's either pissed off at me or thinking I deserve a reward because my hand is cramping by the time the words run dry. I'm itching to start editing it — but I'm dead tired and I wouldn't recognize a masterpiece if it bit me on the ass right now. I shut the notebook with a snap and get up to turn off the light again.

That's when I hear it. The sound of muffled crying. Lilah.

I crack open the door, but she's huddled under the covers, just a curled lump in the middle of the mattress.

Without saying a word, I scoop her up covers and all and take her with me into the closet. She hiccups slightly under there somewhere but doesn't say a word. Not until I settle her down on top of me, anyway.

Then she sort of humphs and squeaks like she doesn't know how to start the conversation. Without even making a conscious decision, I'm ready to offer up my deepest secrets to her.

LILAH

Oh, God. I seem to be in an endless cycle of embarrassment when it comes to Todd. When he left me alone in the enormous bed, in a strange room, since I really don't remember much of the previous night, I felt overwhelmed and out of my depth. Kind of have since I started walking up the hill in all honesty. But something about the dark and the strange pillow had me thinking about all my problems and the coffee shop and not being sure where anything is going.

Most of the time I can stay on the sunny side — a glass half-full perspective, but right this minute, not so much. It's like I've been holding too much in, trying to be a little too brave in the face of disaster and now cracks are spreading across the dam.

The tears started leaking, and I tried to stop them. I did. For a while, they just rolled, and I sniffed a bit. But then I remembered that I'd have to open the shop in two days and how was I going to do that without the help I can't afford on one leg? I don't think you can serve coffee from crutches. Not if you have to move from one end of the bar to the other. And that's when I realized that this was all probably over before it started. Todd doesn't want me living here. Not yet, anyway. Otherwise, why would he be sleeping in the closet? Although it's probably a good thing because then he'd know I'm certifiable lying here crying over nothing in particular.

When he scoops me up, he scares the life out of me. Mostly because I didn't hear him approach and then I'm moving, blankets and all. When we stop and I feel like I'm horizontal again, it takes me a minute to dig out enough to speak. "Todd? What's going on?"

"I was going to ask you the same thing," he says dryly. "Lilah, why are you sobbing like it's the end of the world?"

"I wasn't!" I'm indignant. "That was just a general cry. Sobbing is entirely different."

I can practically feel him shrug with masculine dismissal of the subtleties. "Why, Lilah?"

"Because my life is a mess and I seem to only make it worse?" I mumble.

"Do you really want to know why I have a bed in my closet?"

"Not if you don't want to tell me," I admit. I'm dying of curiosity, but I don't need to pry where there are bruises. Not without a reason to think that's necessary.

He pauses and then seems to come to some decision. "My dad died suddenly when I was really young. Maybe three and a half, probably somewhere closer to four. My mom moved the two of us in with my uncle. Her older half brother. I'm not sure if he offered, or if he just didn't say no when we showed up, but it… it didn't go well."

I can feel the tension in his entire body despite the bundle of blankets between us. "My room wasn't really meant to be a bedroom, I don't think. It wasn't big, and it was downstairs next to the kitchen. It had this funky closet that was built in under the staircase to the upstairs."

Todd swallows convulsively and I wait, dreading what's coming. "My uncle, he wasn't thrilled with me or even tolerant. I'm vague on the details, but I remember him storming into my room and screaming at me. That inevitably led to him beating on me."

"You were four!"

"Yeah, I'm not sure if that made me an easy target or if he had a very low tolerance for kids. I remember one time clearly when he laid into me for not making my bed properly."

I curl my fingers into Todd's chest instinctively, as if it's going to prevent me from socking this man that isn't even here.

"Anyway, my mom was too messed up to do anything. I'm not sure how much of it she was even aware of. Looking back on it, she was probably popping anti-depressants to cope with her grief to the point that murder would have gone unnoticed. But it didn't take me long to figure out that I was small and my uncle was big and the closet was narrower at the back. And after one time that he started whaling on me when I was still asleep I moved into the closet."

"What did he do then?"

Todd huffs out a laugh that's not amusement. "Nothing that I recall. My official bed stayed made, and I spent any time that my uncle was in the house or I was asleep curled up with my stuffed animals as far back as I could get. Then my other uncle, the one that lives here, came for a visit. He's my dad's oldest brother. According to him, he took one look at my room and knew something was off. When he looked in the closet, he said it stank to high heaven and he wasn't leaving me alone there another night. He hustled me and my mom into a hotel and then brought us back here."

"You grew up here? I don't recall reading that." I sound disgruntled, like my recent cyber stalking has been found out to be subpar.

Todd gives a genuine chuckle this time. "Relax, sexy coffee shop girl who didn't recognize the rock star. No, I didn't. Uncle Lou got Mom some help and me too, for that matter. We lived with him for a couple of years and then Mom met her current husband. He lived in San Francisco, so we moved there the summer before I started second grade."

"And what was he like? Did you move right back into a new closet?"

I can feel Todd shift beneath me. "He's fine. Bit of a boring office manager, but he treats my mom well, and he never did more than raise his voice to me as a teenager, which I usually deserved. Uncle Lou checked in on me frequently, and I knew I could always come back here if I needed to. But closets have always felt safe to me, blocks out the outside world, you know?

I saw a therapist for a while as an adult. When I felt that the touring was sending me too close to the edge. And her conclusion was as long as it wasn't interfering with living my life than it was probably always going to be a safe place for me and that's not a bad thing. I do mostly sleep in a regular bed in a regular room, but when I can't sleep or something's bothering me, I get more rest in the closet."

I finally free my arms enough to wrap them around him, as much as I can anyway since I can't really slide them under him with me on top. And I hang on with everything I've got, trying to convey with my hug that I'm so sorry he had such a shitty uncle and that his mom hadn't been there to protect him. "So, what happened to your evil uncle?"

"You may not like this part," he warns.

"It gets worse?" I don't know if I'm shocked or flabbergasted.

"Eh. More poetic revenge on my part. He came searching for me a few years ago. Okay, maybe it's been ten by now. Anyway, he acted like nothing had happened and how happy he was to have been a part of my success."

"You are fucking kidding me!" I'm outraged and try to pull up in anger.

"Relax, baby. I knew he was angling for money, but I also knew he had a drinking problem. So despite desperately wanting to tell him off with every four letter word I knew, I struck a deal with the devil."

"What did you do?" I ask breathlessly. I'm on tenterhooks here.

"I bought his house from him and let him stay there while I pay him in monthly installments on condition that he get random drug and alcohol testing and stay away from the reporters. If he fails one test or talks, he loses everything."

"That's diabolical." And impressive.

"Still going to respect me in the morning?" Todd asks in jest, but I hear the underlying question as to whether I'm thinking he went too far or not far enough.

"If I wasn't in love with you before, I would be now," I mumble quietly.

With a flash of movement Todd reverses our positions, which is seriously impressive given how narrow this bed is. I shriek and then that turns to a moan as his lips descend on mine. When he finally pulls back, it's to say, "Why am I only hearing about this now?"

9

LILAH

The closet smells of warm, comforting cedar. I strain my eyes in the darkness to see anything of Todd's face. Why is he surprised that I love him? Or maybe he's just playing? Somehow my arms have gotten trapped in the blankets again and I can't seem to free them. "Why are you acting shocked?" I finally ask suspiciously.

"Lilah, all women are a mystery to me. You — you're on an entirely new level of intriguing and baffling." Either he can see in the dark or he has unerring radar because his lips find mine without any awkwardness. It's delicious except for the part where I can't raise my arms to tug him closer. I pull my lips away.

"I'm the confusing one? And can you unwrap me so I can move?" I whisper the last part because it's a little silly to be trussed up by a blanket in a celebrity's closet. Then I think about what that would look like on a supermarket tabloid cover and I burst into giggles.

"What's so funny?" Todd asks hesitantly as if he's afraid I've finally lost it and gone over the edge.

"Just thinking about those tabloid headlines in the grocery store, you know? I'm pregnant with an alien ghost's baby or I was held captive by a blanket in a rock star's closet. Hey, maybe the ghost alien baby is real then?" The giggles continue to escape leaving me breathless.

Todd growls and, if anything, pulls the blanket tighter. "If you're going to run to the tabloids, then I guess I'll have to keep you wrapped up for my personal pleasure forever."

"You know I'm kidding, right?" I ask, suddenly anxious. I don't for a minute want him to think I'd ever betray him like that, even if I was pissed off and angry.

He kisses me again. "I do. If that was your game, you'd have done it when I first walked into the coffee shop. Although, you'd have had to recognize me for that," he amends, with laughter in his voice.

I groan. "Are you never going to let me live that down?"

"Nope."

I squirm beneath him, trying once again to get closer. I feel his hands over the blankets and then he swears, "Fuck. The one problem with keeping you trussed like this is I can't reach your pretty pussy."

I giggle at that. "So what are you going to do about it?" I ask archly, genuinely curious to find out.

"Hmmm. I think maybe it's time we went back to the big bed. And then you're going to tell me why you were crying."

Oh that. Damn. The comforting weight of Todd's body disappears and then there's blazing light, making me squint. It's only a dim closet fixture, but the shock from total darkness makes it seem brighter. He scoops me up again and carries me into the comforting shadows of the main bedroom. When I'm fully unraveled of the extra bedclothes, I get back between the cool sheets of the king-size bed. Then Todd is there with me, pressed against my side, his arm pulling me tight. "So why the tears, Lilah?" his tone is quiet but insistent.

I shrug my shoulders against his chest. "It's not one particular thing. Just a lot of stuff rolled together. I feel like a failure when it comes to the coffee shop, despite knowing I'm technically doing more business than my aunt. But somehow that doesn't make me feel better because it's not enough, definitely not to keep it open. And I don't want to leave the island when you're here but it's too soon to..." I wave my hand in the air even though I know he can't see it (unless of course he really can see in the dark) but I can't say the words. It's too presumptuous of me.

"Too soon for what? To say I love you too? Or too soon to move in with me or let me help give back to the community by keeping the coffee shop open?"

"Uhhh, all of the above?"

Todd growls in my ear, "Wrong answer. It's none of the above, pretty girl. All of the above wasn't one of the choices on that particular test question."

I change the topic because neither of us is going to win this argument now. "Are you okay out here? Compared to the closet, that is?"

In response, he kisses me again, deeply and sweetly. "I'm good, baby. I think you give me as much peace as any closet, even when you're being difficult."

I beam with delight from the inside out. That's probably the nicest thing anyone's ever said to me.

"Now go to sleep. We're going to fix all this shit about money in the morning." With that dire threat, he turns over on his stomach, still keeping one arm around my waist and pretend snores.

Jeez. But still I feel warm and included and my thoughts have nowhere to go but happy, which is how I fall asleep.

TODD

I let my right middle finger express my sentiments regarding the four guys arranged at the base of the stairs grinning up at me in disbelief. Lilah is behind me, so she can't see my gesture, but she's grumbling too. No doubt at me, since she has no idea they're being stupid just yet. My left hand is resting on the handrail, only because Lilah insisted — some crazy thought that she could take me down if she fell against me. She's not big enough to do that, but there was no convincing her. Would have been easier if she just let me carry her.

Yes, I'm grumbling. She's too precious to be taking chances. She should stay off that ankle at least another week, nevermind what the nurse said. The nurse is not a doctor. We need a proper physician again on this island, now that the previous one retired (and moved away because he was smart enough to know people would still call him.) A real doctor would tell Lilah to let me take care of her and not take any unnecessary risks.

But Lilah was having none of it, so here we are inching down the stairs because the only way I'd let that happen is if she was behind me with one hand on my shoulder. And we did this one step at a time.

Probably if I were at the bottom looking up, I'd be grinning too, but hopefully I'd have better things to do. I aim that thought directly at the four grown men standing there with matching quizzical expressions. The guys finally move back when we reach the lower stairs to make room. I watch my girl carefully as she limps into the kitchen.

"Sit down, Lilah, please? That's enough for now."

She glances over her shoulder with a pained expression. "For you or for me? You need to relax, Todd. I'm all in one piece."

I scrub my hand over my face, ignoring the bemused expressions of the others. "Don't you guys have something better to do?" I ask sarcastically.

"Nope. Not really. Still mostly on vacation, dude," says Karl. While Ernie chimes in with, "Not as good as this."

Lilah has the fridge door open, so I move through to make sure she knows she's not cooking for this gang.

"Lilah, sit. I'll fix breakfast."

"You can cook?"

"What do you want?"

She hunches her shoulders in confusion, then her eyes take in the others still lounging against the wall. "Um, what do you guys normally do? I know yesterday was pancakes, but I thought that was a special occasion.”

I snort. “Normally they sleep until noon because they claim when they’re here they’re being rock stars and that’s what rock stars do. When they’re home, they don’t have anyone else to feed them. I know for a fact, Roman gets up at five to water his garden before the sun comes up.”

Lilah glances at the small clock on the stove. “It’s only seven?”

Roman takes pity on her. “We’re having too much fun watching TK lose his shit to miss any of it.”

Her eyes go wide. I sigh and point firmly at one of the bar stools. “Coffee will be served when your ass is parked on that chair and not before.”

She looks like she’s going to argue, but then glances at Lance in the corner. She perches on the edge of the stool and folds her hands demurely on the counter.

I nod in approval and swing a mug down from the cupboard, filling it from the carafe on the side. Then I have second thoughts. “Who made the coffee?”

“I did,” Lance says quietly, studying his fingernails. I slide the mug over to Lilah. Karl’s coffee is shit. He knows it, but it’s always better to ask.

I take out enough bacon and an entire carton of eggs. Luckily, I’d had a delivery from the mainland arranged a week ago, knowing that quick and easy food is a necessity when we get in the zone. Nobody wants to stop the magic and by the time it's faded, restaurants are usually closed and we're famished. Plus, the small local grocery doesn't really run to the snobby standards of the organic gardener in the group.

When I've got the bacon lined up on the griddle, I fold my arms and glare at the peanut gallery. "If you guys are just going to stand around all day, you can at least be useful. Group meeting after breakfast."

Ernie is the first to object. "What happened to vacation? And it's Sunday. Meetings are supposed to happen on weekdays."

"Nope. Lilah's shop needs to open in the morning and one of you is going to volunteer. But we'll discuss that *after* breakfast."

Lilah's mouth is the first to open in objection, but she closes it again when I give her a warning glare. She can save her arguments for the meeting too.

LILAH

My sense of being giddy, exhausted, and overwhelmed has only ratcheted up several notches since yesterday. It's that feeling of an invisible giant, steel-toed work boot hanging over my head on a breaking string.

And then there was all the other emotional upheaval of the night — I need to process that. Take some time to think through everything I learned and how I'm handling my own situation. On top of that, it's all coming with an audience of four curious strangers. They seem like decent guys, but I don't know them really and yet here we all are ready for breakfast on Sunday morning.

It's a lot to take in. There's only a small table in the kitchen, so two of the guys sit there while Todd glares at me every time I even think about getting off the bar stool at the island. The other two men take up positions on the remaining bar stools at the corner while Todd remains standing on the kitchen side of the island, even after everyone has food on their plate. "We could go into the dining room?" I ask hesitantly, not wanting him to have to stand for the entire meal just because his friends are clueless.

"I'm good, love." Todd smiles gently while Karl turns slightly to stare at the two of us. He turns back to his plate without saying a word.

Deciding to follow his example and focus on my breakfast, I take a nibble of bacon and then moan with pleasure. This isn't ordinary bacon. It's bacon at an entirely new level. I eye the rest of the strip in my hand with puzzlement, wondering what makes it so spectacular. The silence draws my attention up. Five sets of eyes are watching me with varying levels of amusement. Except the pair staring directly down at me. Todd's gaze is a mix of heat and annoyance. I raise my eyebrows at him. Instead of responding, he glares at his friends. What was that all about?

I nibble some more, but this time I'm careful to hold in the sound effects. Such a pity, but I guess it's worth it when I see Todd relax back enough to start eating.

"So how come nobody brought their wives or girlfriends, if this is also a vacation?" I ask curiously, only just noticing that fact.

Todd snorts with derision. "Because they're all painfully single. Do *not* offer to fix them up. They're all hopeless."

It's on my tip of my tongue to ask *even you*? But I bite it back. Instead, I keep my attention on my scrambled eggs. The silence is a tiny bit awkward, to me at least. But nobody else seems bothered, so I try to let it go.

10

LILAH

The guys eat like... well, guys. For the most part, they keep their eyes on their plates, with a few mumbled exchanges when a thought pops into one of their graying heads. There's a clatter as they almost simultaneously finish and drop their utensils down on their plates. I'm still nibbling my last piece of toast, but I start to stand so I can take my dishes to the sink. Instead, they're whisked out from under me and Todd's face is looming close to mine.

"Stay put, Lilah. You need at least an hour with your foot elevated before you walk on it again."

"Says who?" I gasp at him in astonishment. The nurse never said anything of the sort.

"I did some research."

I roll my eyes at that one. But if he wants to gather dirty dishes, who am I to stop him? A minute later, without warning, he's scooping me up in his favorite move and carrying me into the sunken living room. He sets me down on the couch before sliding an upholstered ottoman under my bad leg. Then he spends an entire minute adjusting a throw pillow so that my leg is raised to the height he thinks it should be. It's a bit overkill, but secretly I can admit it does feel better.

The rest of the band wander in behind us and take perches, leaning against the wall or on the opposite sofa.

"Okay, TK, what's this about then?"

"Lilah owns the coffee shop in town. It's a vital part of the community and obviously she can't be running around fixing drinks in her condition."

I stare at Todd from under my lashes. Vital part of the community? With three customers on a good day in the winter? And why is everyone staring at me…? I blush hard. "For the record, I'm not pregnant and maybe the coffee shop should just stay closed. This might be a more graceful exit than admitting to everyone that it's not making any money." I bravely stare down Todd with this statement. But surprisingly that seems to get the other guys motivated.

"What do you mean, it's not making money? How is that even possible with coffee in the Pacific Northwest?"

I'm not entirely sure who said that. I was too busy not blinking first while trying to remain unyielding under Todd's baleful glare, but I do eventually switch my attention to the rest of the room.

"There aren't enough customers in the winter to pay for the sugar that they all swipe."

"Okay if I take a look?" Lance asks, almost bashfully.

"Uh…"

Todd softly adds, "Lance was a competition-winning barista before we hit it big. He does know what he's talking about."

"Then, I guess?" I'm embarrassed that I'm taking favors from someone with two successful careers when I can't even claim one.

"No offense to you or your shop, Lilah, but what about the album?" Karl speaks up firmly from the corner of the room where he's lounging against the wall and looking out the window.

Todd leans forward eagerly, like he was waiting for this question. "Why don't we push everything back two weeks? I already checked with Carlos and that schedule works better for him, anyway."

Roman straightens from his slouch. "Now hold on, we aren't all on permanent vacation here."

Todd rolls his eyes. "Why don't you just invite Lottie to come here? Maybe then she'll figure out how you feel about her."

The taller man glares at Todd. "She's my housekeeper, nothing else. Have some respect."

Todd stares in disbelief. "I do, man. She's perfect for you. But not if she keeps living in the pool house. You need to put a ring on it."

I swear a blush sweeps over the other man. "Well… maybe a few more weeks away might make her miss me. A little…" He looks uncertain and suddenly I can't see these guys as famous rock stars. They're lonely and they need help. I straighten up, ready to right the world and solve everyone's problems.

"Okay, Lance, maybe you and I can go down to the shop this afternoon and I'll show you where everything is?"

He nods and Todd glares. "What?" I ask him with exasperation.

"I'm coming too."

"Why?" I'm genuinely perplexed.

"Because I don't want anyone else holding you," he grumbles in my ear with a rasp that does something to my insides.

"Anybody else have any objections?" Todd finally asks when he pulls back.

There are a few shrugs but nobody says anything. "Fine, then that's settled. I'll tell Carlos and order in some more food."

"Who's Carlos?" I ask as the guys start filing out of the room.

"Sound engineer," Karl tells me with a small smile. He's the only one I haven't heard anything personal about, so I wonder what his story is?

TODD

I dust off one of the fancier cars to take Lilah down to her shop. I can't even remember what it is, something Italian I think. But more importantly, it has room for three people and it runs. I have a mechanic stop by every six months and keep things in working order. That's still not enough to make the classic Jaguar reliable, but it does look pretty in the garage.

Lilah insists on walking out the front door on her own. She's got the crutches with her at least, but I think she's only using them for balance if she falters.

She frowns at me when I open the back door for her. "Why don't I get to ride up front? Is it because I'm female or because I'm the youngest?"

"Because you should stretch your leg out," I tell her without remorse.

Lilah glares half-heartedly, but scoots in and hands me the crutches, which I set in the immaculate trunk. (Proof that I never drive this thing.)

Starting the engine, I tap the horn to remind Lance to get the hell out here. Naturally, it takes another five minutes during which I have to endure Lilah's breathless little giggles as she pushes buttons on the rear control panel and waits to see what they'll do. It's making me hard, and it's going to be hours before I can do anything about it.

Finally, Lance comes bounding out of the house, looking exactly the same as the last time I saw him. "What the hell took you so long?" I grouse.

He smiles benignly. "Just checking on some promotion dates with Roman. Seeing where we can loop the coffee shop in."

Lilah's voice is hesitant when she finally speaks up. "Lance... I don't want you guys giving me special favors. I appreciate it, but..."

He turns and gives her a soft smile that has me clenching my fists on the steering wheel as I navigate down the hill. "Relax, Lilah. It's not a big deal. We all like coming to the island and we want it to stay the way it is. Sending fans into a coffee shop is really for us — keeps them off TK's porch."

"I don't have a damn porch," I spit out between my clenched teeth.

"What's the matter now?" Lance sounds downright bewildered. When I don't answer, he glances back at Lilah, who I can see rolling her eyes in response via the rear-view mirror.

"I thought now that you weren't caging the monkey

you'd be more relaxed." I can feel his eyes scanning me from the passenger seat. "Ohhhh, is that the problem? Things not as responsive as they once were?"

Between Lance's loose mouth and Lilah's snort-laugh-cough from the backseat, I've had enough. I stop the car in the middle of the road and turn so I can glare at both of them.

"What the hell, Lance? Caging the monkey? What does that even mean?" I hold up my hand when I see his mouth open. "No. I don't think I want to know." I swivel my eyes to Lilah. "And for the record, everything is in working order."

I see a brief flash of anxiety flash across her face, but she hides it fast. I sigh — not what I wanted to go into in front of Big Mouth. "Lilah. Not since before you came to the island. Got it?"

She dips her chin ever so slightly in acknowledgment, her eyes peeking at me through her lashes with a gleam I'd like to explore in more detail. Unfortunately, Lance also understood what I was saying. "The rest of us cramping your style, TK? My sister is always saying she has a shy bladder and needs the house to herself to pee. We can skedaddle for a few hours, if that will help." He sound genuinely concerned so I don't slap him upside the head like I want to. Lilah is fighting the giggles again. Biting her lip until the indentation turns white while her eyes fill with mirth.

I give up. I start the car moving again while heaving one of those exasperated dad sighs. Considering I don't have kids, or even nieces and nephews, it's amazing how easily it comes.

LILAH

I don't know how, seeing as he's also about twenty years older than me, but Lance feels like the little brother I never knew I wanted. Now that I've found him, though, I'm keeping him. I learn so much more when he's in the room! I eye the back of Todd's neck with interest. I thought we'd hashed everything out about our feelings? Or at least enough not to have a reason to wait any longer. Unless he's trying to be a gentleman and waiting for me to make the first move? I can do that.

Then I think back to whatever *that* was in his office yesterday. There were rules alright, but not the kind found in any etiquette book. I thoroughly enjoyed it too. Until Todd disappeared on me because he didn't think I was ready for all the heavy emotional stuff. Or something. I don't think we need to save fucking for when we've worked out every possible complication in our relationship. I suppose it's nice that he doesn't want me to feel like he's using me because I'm convenient. But seriously, who could possibly think I'm *convenient* after all the trouble I've caused in the last few days? And I'm still going to respect him in the morning…

So tonight then? I try not to burn a hole in the back of his head with my eyes. For one thing, forewarning him of my plans might give him too much of an advantage.

Look at me, plotting how to seduce a rock star! As long as it's Todd, of course. I've no real interest in any others, but I'm still proud of myself for being so far out of my comfort zone. We don't need to talk about my one brief boyfriend — if you could even call him that. I never slept with him, but we were each other's pity dates for about six months. I kept hoping I'd start to feel something more for him, but there was never even a glimmer. He sold orthopedic insoles. With passion and commitment. Do you really need to hear more than that?

It shouldn't come as a surprise then, that all those months when Todd came into the coffee shop with easy grace had me tongue-tied and afraid of making some terrible gaffe. Which, obviously, happened anyway. And yet here I am. Proof that miracles really can happen.

Todd parks the car right in front of the shop. Not something I'd encourage if it were open, but it's definitely easier to navigate through the wider plate-glass door than the one in the alley. He upends a few stools from a table and places them by the front counter. He frowns at me until I slide onto one of them with a sigh. Lance hangs back, his hands in his front pockets, eyes bouncing around the sunlit interior. Todd starts playing with my left hand, idly sliding his fingers back and forth between mine, while I wait for some kind of verdict from the band's coffee expert.

Lance walks behind the counter, studies the espresso machine briefly before turning his attention to the large chalkboard that holds the brief menu. I watch his shoulders sag. He glances over one of them at me. "Can I change this? Please?" He's practically pleading.

My first reaction is to say no. That the town won't stand for change. But before the words come out, I realize that it really doesn't matter. If the three customers that might come in on a good day are offended and leave, it won't affect the outcome.

"Sure," I say with a light shrug, denying the anxiety that's crawling at my belly. Todd's arm curls around my waist as he leans against my back.

"Such a good girl, being open to new experiences," he whispers in my ear with a wicked drawl. Even though I can't see it, I can hear the smirk plain as day and it has me shifting uncomfortably in my seat, suddenly aware of how close he is.

I lightly smack his arm in retaliation, but he merely tightens his hold in response. Lance seems oblivious to us. While I was distracted, he went and found the folding stepstool I keep in the back and is now busy cleaning off the entire chalkboard.

Twenty minutes later, I'm staring at the new menu in shock. Eight dollars for a… I don't even know how to pronounce it… assaporetto? Which, according to Lance's carefully chalked words, features high notes of caramel and burnt sugar. "Uh, isn't that going to need special ingredients? I've only got what's on the counter or in the back. They just stock the basics at the grocery."

Lance grins and his face transforms into the one I recognize from all the band's PR. "It's all in the marketing, Lilah. It's just regular espresso with lots of milk and a pump of caramel syrup and some brown sugar. One of the cheapest things to make, really."

"Oh."

"Look down at the left bottom corner. That's for the conservative locals."

I look. It says *coffee $1.50, coffee with hot milk $1.75* "But that's even less…?"

He nods. "It is, but that's only for the real penny-pinchers who will complain about the extra fluff, anyway. Most everyone is going to want to treat themselves to something fancy. Now for the problem of sugar walking out the door."

Lance sounds full of enthusiasm and excitement. I study him as he goes around collecting the little boxes of sugar packets and then dumps them in a drawer behind the counter. My eyes are getting wider. He swings into the back room and emerges with a small table that's been sitting back there for forever with no real purpose. He sets it in front of one of the side windows where there's a gap in the tables. "You said there's a grocery in town?"

"Yes, one street back between here and the main part of the village, but what do you need?"

His smirk is like a pesky little brother too, the one that knows he's smarter than you. "Sugar." And with that, he heads out the door with a cheerful wave.

11

TODD

I have an idea what Lance has planned, but honestly, it's not that important to me. I'm more intrigued by Lilah's puzzled face. "If you weren't running a coffee shop, what would you be doing for a career?" I'm genuinely curious because while her sunny smile is a perfect fit, I think she was probably made for bigger and brighter things.

She grimaces. "I don't know. I majored in comparative literature for no particular reason other than I like to read and I enjoyed those professors' classes. It's not a natural gateway into jobs in the real world, though. Not when you have to explain what it is in every interview."

"So, what is it?" She left me an opening I'm not embarrassed to take. It sounds like something I ought to know, but I barely remember anything about school beyond the small smoky venues we felt lucky to get as gigs. I probably wouldn't have even bothered graduating if our big break had happened two weeks earlier.

"The study of human communication across cultures and forms," she says like she's reading off of a brochure. "But really, for me, there was one professor that was really into the myths and stories that are shared by unconnected cultures around the world. Like origin stories that start with an explosion. It was so interesting to consider how and why that might be. Is it deeply buried in our human psyche or some kind of ancestral memory?"

I sure as hell don't have the answer to that, but I'm basking in her glow because she seems genuinely fascinated by the question.

"But, that's ancient history at this point. Anyway, you were asking about my jobs. Mostly low-paying office work that was boring as hell. I can't even blame other people for that because I could never articulate what I wanted to be doing. I honestly don't know. Surely I should have that nailed and be moving up the ladder by now. You knew what you wanted, right? I'm sure the other guys did too or you wouldn't have made it. I thought my aunt's bequest was the answer to everything when it happened. Except while it's kept me busy, it doesn't feel like a life purpose."

"Hmm," I say as noncommittally as I can manage. I know what her life purpose is, but she'd probably take offense if I told her it involved getting fucked by me on a very regular basis. Maybe if I start slowly showing her instead? I'm just about to suggest I carry her up to her apartment when Lance comes tromping back in with a cheerful whistle and a five-pound bag of supermarket sugar. There's an additional small brown paper bag looped over his arm.

Lilah's face is a study in bewilderment as she tracks Lance's movements to the counter, then the sink, and finally, as he starts pouring sugar from the bag into the glass canisters he's just washed. He winks at her. "No more stealing sugar."

"But I tried sugar bowls when I moved here. It didn't go down well. I thought there might be a riot."

"Let me guess, you used some kind of fancy sugar?" Lance waits for her answer with a raised eyebrow and a smirk.

"Well, yes. Turbinado is healthier, sort of," she admits with a frown.

"And therein lies your problem. Basic, familiar processed sugar is what this crowd is after. It looks like the sugar they're used to."

"And they won't just empty it at the first opportunity?" Lilah still sounds skeptical and I want to kiss the anxiety from her.

"Naw, there's going to be so much sugar in those drinks already, more won't dissolve. Wait and see."

This is the most confident I've seen Lance in a long time. He's quick to go into the zone in the studio, but that doesn't involve talking, or at least not much. He sets up the small table he dragged in earlier with the sugar and some other odds and ends. He wipes down the counter and throws the towel in the hamper by the sink like he's worked in this cafe all his life. "Right. I think I'm good for the morning. Anything else?"

"Um, the cash register?"

Lance quickly hits a few buttons without even looking, and the cash drawer shoots open. "Know this model, no problems Li — we need a nickname for you."

"What the fuck? Lilah is too long for you to manage?" I glare at him pissily.

He grins in response. "Everyone should have a nickname for close friends, yeah?"

Lilah laughs, "Really, it's okay, Lance. I've always been just Lilah."

Now I'm frowning at her. "You're not *just* anything, baby. But I don't think you need to be so close to Lance that it requires a nickname."

She purses her lips at me. "Are you jealous? Of my new honorary little brother?"

"He's twenty years older than you!"

"Not really." She shrugs dismissively with a sweet smile while I can hear Lance snickering in the background. Maybe she has a point.

"Lance, you can walk home," I tell him without turning my head. Time to make sure Lilah understands a few things. I know I said we should wait until she trusted in our future together but the need to claim her and *show* her the depth of my feelings for her is overwhelming. I hold her gaze while she sobers and gulps before reaching a hand out to rest on my lower arm. It stays there, warm and inviting, like she simply needs to be touching me. Nothing could make me happier, but I need more of her.

"Right. I can take a hint," Lance mumbles as if he's talking to himself and he might as well be. I hear him head for the door. "Don't forget to lock up, kids," he says a little too loudly before the door swings shut with a tinkle of bells. Lilah leans in closer. "What are you waiting for, Mr. Kipling?"

"Not one damn thing. But you stay put while I lock the front and open up the back. You are not going up those stairs under your own power. They're too steep."

She rolls her eyes but stays put. Good, she's learning.

LILAH

By the time Todd returns to where I'm sitting, I've worked myself into a fine state of nerves. I know I talked big about seducing my rock star just a few hours ago, but... I also know what little sexual experience I have is small-town potatoes and nothing to write home about — even in a small town. I'm not a virgin, but I might as well be because my sexual encounters in college were not only brief but unsatisfying. I didn't see the point in trying again without a deeper emotional connection. That well runs so deep with Todd that I could lose myself in him.

Todd's movements are brisk and efficient as he crosses the cafe to me, but his gaze is searching. He leans down, his lips tantalizingly close to mine. "Trust me, Lilah?"

I nod jerkily, unsure exactly what I'm signing up for, but determined not to miss out. Not when it comes to him.

His smile is tight. "Sorry about this, but the stairs are too narrow to do it any other way."

That's all the warning I get before he scoops me and throws me over his shoulder. Then he's striding through the back, stopping just inside the doorway. "Get the door, would you, Lilah?"

"Seriously?" I ask with a grumble. But I reach an arm out and pull the door shut. He takes the stairs slowly. I hope that's because he doesn't want me to bounce and not because I'm too heavy. "I really can walk, you know."

A growl is his only response. Then he tips me over onto the bed, keeping his hand on my legs, I guess so I don't hit my injured ankle. I sit up just enough to realize what a mess I left the place in before I headed out on Friday afternoon. I groan and flop back down. "This place is a mess."

"Only see you, baby."

I grin at that with my eyes closed. "That line will get you out of a lot of trouble, mister. Hang on to it."

"And what line will get you out of those clothes?"

That makes my eyes pop wide open. He's staring down at me, his hands jammed into the front pockets of his jeans as if he doesn't trust himself not to touch.

"Todd?"

"Hmm?" His gaze flicks up to meet mine.

"Could you maybe… I mean, I'd like it if…" I stumble over the words I want to say while Todd rocks back on his heels, his eyes holding a speculative gleam.

I flush with awkwardness. Finally, he takes pity on me. "Lilah, you can have whatever you want, sweetness. What is it?" He gentles his voice, which just embarrasses me more. I'm a grown-ass woman. I should be able to ask for what I want in the bedroom, right?

"I-want-you-to-be-in-charge-so-I-don't-have-to-think-and-mess-everything-up," I wheeze out in a single frantic breath before covering my face with my hands. I watch Todd blink several times through my spread fingers. Then a slow smile pulls at his gorgeous lips.

"Let me see if I heard that correctly," he practically purrs. "You're inviting me to have my wicked way with you? Anything goes?"

I drop my hands to stare at him, my eyes wide. "Anything?" I squeak.

"Did I misunderstand?" he challenges me.

"Nooo, but my anything is probably a lot tamer than yours," I admit.

That makes him laugh outright. "How about this, anything my grandmother would have at least heard of."

I eye him suspiciously.

"She was a very nice old lady. She died about fifteen years ago."

Still not entirely sure where he's drawing the limit but impatient to get on with it, I nod.

Todd stills, then leans over the bed and trails a

finger down the line of my throat. "Did I mention that my grandmother lived a very bohemian lifestyle in the Village before she married my grandfather?" I know he's teasing me, but I still gulp.

He claims my lips before I can hope to get a word out. I drink him in, eager to be overwhelmed. But rather than dive deeper, he pulls back.

"Fuck, Lilah, you are too sweet for your own good. I need to be inside you so badly, I'm not sure how good I can make this for you — the first time. But I'll make it up to you later. I promise."

"Later?" My voice falters, wondering if he means some unnamed time in the future like oh, next week.

He grimaces. "Round two, baby. Give or take twenty to thirty minutes from now. Does that work for you?"

Can't we just get on with it? My impatience must be written on my face because Todd's goes all stern. "Turn over."

"What? Why?"

"Because I said so? And you just asked me to take charge."

"Oh." So, I did. Slowly and without taking my eyes off his face until I absolutely have to, I roll over onto my stomach.

TODD

I wasn't kidding when I told Lilah that I might not be able to last. She's so damn sweet, I want to lick every inch of her. And someday I'm going to do exactly that, but not today. Her breathing is stilted and her fingers are clenching the sheet like she needs to hang on. I shake my head and try to think what's going to get her to relax.

If I had any doubts that she wanted to be here, I'd carry her back downstairs and drive her home without a word of reproach. But I recognize first time nerves when I see them. Not that I've experienced that in decades. Until now. I want this to be mind-blowing for Lilah. So good, any doubts she has about a future with me or spending my money will dissolve and disappear forever.

She's wearing some kind of slinky dark yoga pants and a long shirt, but the top has bunched up around her waist, leaving me free to admire the perfect curve of her ass.

"What's taking so long?" she grumbles without turning her head.

"Who's in charge here?" I tap that ass lightly with the flat of my hand.

"You are," she concedes with a heavy sigh that makes me chuckle.

"Then lift that lovely ass. As much as I like looking at you in those pants, they're definitely in the way."

She raises her lower body and I skim the pants down and off, leaving them tangled around her ankles. Repeating the process with her simple cotton panties, I watch a blush spread up her body. "Are you blushing because I just found out how wet your panties are?" I guess curiously.

"Maybe," she admits into the sheet.

"They are awfully wet," I muse, sliding a finger through her folds. "Were you thinking about this down in the cafe? Or even earlier?"

"When am I not thinking about it?" she grouses adorably.

"Hmmm. Turn over again. I have a new plan."

"What was the old one?" she inquires as she rolls over onto her back. She starts to sit up, reaching for her ankles, but I stop her forward progress. "Nope, pants stay where they are. I don't want you flinging that injured ankle about."

"But then…"

I simply raise both eyebrows and wait for her to stop analyzing.

"Oh, right. You're in charge." She rolls her eyes like I was the one that requested that.

Instead of arguing, I reach over and tug her shirt over her head. Finally, I get to see my girl naked when I can savor it. Her skin is still tinged pink from her earlier blush. Her bra barely contains her generous curves and I want it gone. Now.

Lilah must read my mind because she reaches back and undoes the clasp. Her breasts tumble free, round and heavy. My hands itch, eager to test their weight in my palms.

12

LILAH

Todd is trying to kill me here — there's no other obvious explanation. Not only am I the only one that's naked, but apparently I'm also alone in being so aroused as to be almost frantic.

"Todd," I say ominously as he leans over me and kisses a line down my stomach, stopping just short of where I really need his touch.

"Hmm?" he finally responds, clearly distracted.

"Hurry up."

That catches his attention and his laughing eyes meet my glaring ones.

"I sense some interesting sentences in your future, Ms. Mitchell," he drawls with a smirk. "Didn't anyone tell you that the really good things in life should never be rushed?"

My hiss of exasperation expresses my feelings about that quite adequately, I think.

With an exaggerated sigh, Todd slides one and then two fingers into me, making me wriggle with delight. Finally! My pussy flutters and clenches, grateful to have something to fill the void. I reach to pull all of him down on me, wanting his weight surrounding me, pressing me into the mattress. But he resists, instead claiming my lips again while curling and twisting his fingers. He hits that elusive spot and my body jerks violently, convulsing with an orgasm that has me gasping in shock. Todd swallows my cries, his tongue distracting me as his fingers continue to do magical things.

When he finally pulls back just a little, I'm breathless. Not to mention a mess. My thighs are wet and I don't think I could move if a fire burst out right next to me.

"Now you're about ready for me," Todd announces with a perfectly straight face.

He stands and strips his t-shirt over his head. I can feel my body start to revive from a gelatinous blob at the sight of his abs. The man hasn't let himself go in the slightest. But it's when he lowers his jeans that I lick my lips. Only I need to know that instinctive reaction is partly due to nerves. He's huge!

Naturally, this is the moment my mouth goes off on its own tangent. "You went commando? Doesn't that hurt? With the zipper and all?"

Todd looks momentarily bewildered before

realization dawns in his eyes. He leans down and gives me a soft kiss. "Relax, Lilah. I promise you can take all of me like the good girl you are. You're so wet, you may not even notice."

I swallow convulsively, his teasing not enough to make his cock look smaller or less… determined.

"Slide down a little, so your hips are on the edge of the bed and then come up on your elbows. I want you to watch," he instructs me with a note of authority that I find really, really sexy. I do as he said, still not convinced this will work, but beyond intrigued.

When he steps between my bent legs, my ankles still bound by my pants, I can feel my whole body tense with eager anticipation.

"Watch my cock, Lilah," his order grabs my attention from the strained lines of his face.

Obediently, I look down at the purple head poised between my thighs. I can't hold back the groan as I watch it disappear while simultaneously feeling it press into me, widening, invading — the narrow spread of my thighs increasing the pressure.

The onslaught is slow and delicious. I'm full, so full, but I also feel like a piece of me that's always been missing has finally slotted into place. When I can no longer see the space between our bodies, I switch my focus to watching Todd's face. The agony of ecstasy might describe his grimace of concentration. His eyes stare blindly and his breathing is labored.

"You're so fucking tight," he finally manages to utter before pulling out, almost completely, but not quite. His strokes increase in intensity until he's pounding into me, my pussy trying and failing to keep up, to clamp down strong enough to hold him in place. She gets what she wants finally when, with a savage growl, Todd thrusts hard and deep. And stops.

His cum spurts in long ropes deep within me as my pussy finally grips him in a firm hold, milking him for all he's worth. My walls pulse with delight and when Todd suddenly shifts ever so slightly, sliding against my clit, I erupt. I tighten around him like a vise as the pressure bursts — pulsing energy radiating out from my core until even my fingertips are tingling.

Todd's breathing is heavy, his strong arms braced on the bed to either side of me. "Mine, Lilah," he finally pants, his eyes closed. "You're fucking mine."

My pussy clamps down just a little tighter in response and he smiles. I think he knows I just claimed him right back, but there's no way I'll get those words out in my current state of exhausted bliss.

TODD

Truth is, the only music I'm interested in right now involves the sweet sighs and moans Lilah makes when I'm pushing into her. I want more of that. I'm desperate for more of her. I don't really give a fuck about the guys or the album. If it wasn't for Ernie's mom, I'd tell them to go away and come back again in about five years. With a groan of regret, I disengage our bodies so she can breathe. Lilah makes a small sound of distress and her eyes fly open. I kiss them closed again. "Relax, sweetness. I'm trying not to crush you. I'm not done with you yet."

That earns me a tiny smile. "We could stay here…?" she whispers.

"We could. Or I can take you back and hold you captive in my room. Which reminds me…"

"What?" Lilah asks with trepidation.

"You have sentences to do and I've just thought of a way to make it more interesting. So, do you want to do them here or back at the house?"

"How interesting?" Her voice is full of suspicion.

I slide down a little so I can kiss her shoulder. "I'm thinking this time you should sit on my cock while you write."

A slightly glazed look comes over her. "Is that even physically possible?"

Her innocence is addictive. I nod emphatically. "It is. Here or there?"

"Here. Definitely here. But um…" She glances around the small apartment. "I don't exactly have a desk in here."

I give her a smacking kiss on the lips. "I love how agreeable you are to seeing your punishment through, baby."

She rolls her eyes at me. "Would it make any difference if I wasn't?"

I consider that. "Maybe. I think if you really weren't open to letting me protect you, we wouldn't be here. Now, how about a lap desk or even a large book?"

Lilah flops back against the pillows. "There's a lap desk tucked in the corner by the bookcase. Paper and pens are in the top left drawer in the kitchen. This is your idea, you can do the fetching."

Sliding out of bed, I gather the supplies. The longer we talk about it, the more eager I am to see her squirm on my lap. Odds are this will backfire on me just as bad as last time, but that was fun too. Can't lose here, really. I finally help her remove those yoga pants — which I'll never be able to look at again without getting hard — and lean back against the low headboard of the bed.

I have really great ideas. That's the thought going through my head as I help Lilah slide down on my erect cock until she's fully seated and then arrange the lap desk over her knees. It does make it a little harder to reach her clit. But this time seeing as she's completely naked, I can more easily fondle her hard little nipples while she writes. Lilah gives a little wriggle that cascades down the length of my cock, ending in a groan of satisfaction on my part.

"You're a strange man, Todd Kipling," she says dryly, picking up the pen.

"But a happy one. Now write, 'I promise to always keep Todd's cock warm in my perfect pussy.' Notice that I'm letting you off easy since your paper doesn't have as many lines on it."

She snorts softly. I don't know if it was over the sentence or my concession, but she starts writing. I'm slightly disconcerted that her handwriting flows perfectly despite the fact that I'm teasing her breasts with my fingers. When she starts reading, my cock thickens and twitches like it has ears of its own and likes what she's saying.

"How come this is so easy for you this time?" I finally ask when she finishes and I'm starting to sweat with the required restraint not to flip her over and pound into her.

She peers at me over her shoulder and must see something of my struggles because a tiny smile twitches at the corner of her mouth. That's the only warning I get before she clamps her inner walls down on my cock and my vision goes white.

"I think the shock value has worn off. And besides, you aren't the only one with fantasies."

That gets my attention. "Then your next sentence is *my number one fantasy about Todd is…* and fill in the blank."

She pauses for what seems like forever on that one, chewing lightly on the end of the pen. Then her pussy flutters on my cock as she begins to write. My eyes track her words as if my life depends on it…. *to wake up every morning to his smile.* Damn, she's too sweet. Seriously too good for the likes of a grumpy bastard like me. I'm keeping her, anyway.

As soon as she's done writing, I sweep the small plastic desk and paper to the floor and flip her over. "You can say them later. Right now I need to show you something else," I say hoarsely.

"What's that?" Instinctively, she grips my hips with her thighs.

"That you were made for me and I want to make sure you're right here under me every morning when I wake up. That's the only way to make your fantasy come true."

She smiles then. Warm and wide and wraps everything she has around me. I lose myself in her with a roar, determined to explore every inch of her and know her completely. It could take a lifetime.

Unfortunately, we're going to have to clean up and return to the real world before someone, probably Lance, sends out a search party. I'll share my house and my food with the guys, but Lilah is and will remain strictly off limits.

"Do we have to?" she inquires as I carry her into the shower.

"What? Get clean or go back to the house?"

"The house. What if I tied *you* to the bed and kept you captive?" Lilah's attempt at a leer has me grinning with delight.

"Not today, baby. You don't have any food in this place, I looked." I frown down at her, worried all over again that she's let money get in the way of taking proper care of herself.

13

LILAH

I'm deliciously sore and tingly in so many places by the time I limp carefully back into Todd's mansion. The guys are nowhere to be seen, so that probably means they're down practicing. I momentarily feel guilty for keeping their lead singer occupied with other things.

Todd doesn't seem to share that though, because he's hovering — again. "Go find your friends. I'm fine, really. I think I'll take another shower since we didn't really wash in the last one and then maybe do that internet research." I push him towards the door of the bedroom where he likes to deposit me after carrying me up the stairs.

"Are you sure you don't want to…"

I don't let him finish that sentence. "Todd. I'm sure. Go."

He leans down for a kiss that has me melting and almost changing my mind. But I think I'd better work up to all-day sex orgies. His sigh holds more satisfaction than regret as he steps away.

I take my time in the shower. Who wouldn't when given the option of seventeen different water cascades and a voice activated temperature control? When I realize my fingertips have wrinkled like prunes, I reluctantly turn the water off. I wonder how long it takes before having a shower like this becomes normal to the point where I wouldn't give it a second thought?

I curl up on the big bed with my laptop and stack all the pillows around me so I have a cozy nest. Then I start going through the commercial real-estate listings to see what the market looks like. An hour later, I shut down the computer. The market is solid, not hot exactly. Things are moving, but from what I could see not much above asking price and those prices are pretty much middle of the road. I won't get wealthy selling the coffee shop, but it will give me a foundation for starting over. But doing what exactly? And here with Todd? Or is the novelty going to wear off for him before too long? I hate that I'm even thinking that, but... I'm the one that landed on his doorstep, not the other way around.

Chewing on my lip, I have an internal debate with myself as I head downstairs. Dinner preparations are already underway, apparently. Roman directs two of the guys chopping vegetables while he stirs something that smells delicious in a large pan.

"That smells good!" I announce my presence as cheerfully as I can muster. Roman turns his head and acknowledges me with a nod. His eyes are kind, like he can sense my mental unease. "Lilah, better take a seat before TK has a coronary."

"Can't I help?"

"We're good. Almost done with the prep work. Not allergic to anything, are you?"

I shake my head no and help myself to a glass of red wine from the open bottle. It's already dark outside, so there's nothing to see out the windows. Instead, I perch on one of the bar stools and study millionaires cooking their own dinner. It's kind of fascinating.

Todd wanders in, looking a little distracted, but his eyes soften when they land on me. Dinner this time is served in the actual dining room. I've no idea what brought about the change, but it's interesting to see them lined up on either side of the table.

"So none of you have servants? Like a cook or something back home?" I ask curiously because if I had their kind of money, I would gladly hand over the chopping and stirring.

Karl smirks with a wicked twist to his lips. "Roman has a housekeeper. Sort of. The rest of us, no, or at least they're not admitting it."

Roman frowns and glares at Karl. "Lottie is…" he pauses like he's not sure how to finish that sentence.

Ernie helps him out with a grin. "Yes, Lottie is what exactly, Roman? Not your housekeeper?"

Roman swings his glare to the other side of the table. "Lottie is special and not up for discussion."

I stuff a forkful of spaghetti into my mouth so I won't say anything that would increase the awkwardness of the moment.

The mood though shifts back to normal all on its own. Almost like this is a regular thing and the guys start talking about throwing a birthday party for Ernie's mom after she's settled into her new assisted living facility. Todd looks over at me and winks, which makes me blush. There's no doubt in my mind that he's remembering my comments about the band chasing nurses.

But the rest of them don't know that. (Dear God, I hope they don't know that!) Lance stops with his fork in mid air. "What are you two doing over there? No hanky-panky at the dinner table." Todd throws a dinner roll at him, which he catches neatly.

I open my mouth to explain and then shut it again with a sigh. Spelling it out for them would only make things worse.

TODD

Lilah's gone quiet and I can't tell if she's simply tired or if something is on her mind. I herd her upstairs as soon as I can to find out. That, and to get her naked again because now that I've had a taste, I'm already addicted.

"Todd?" The only thing that could drag me away from studying her now naked breasts is Lilah herself.

"Hmm?" I take one perfect rosebud into my mouth to discover if it tastes as sweet as it looks.

"Todd, did you… oh, God… if I hadn't…" her voice trails off as I tongue her rosy nipple into a stiff peak. But now her words have caught my attention more fully, not to mention my curiosity. Pulling back with a slightly regretful sigh, I run my tongue absently over my lips because she does taste like honey. I search her face for some hint as to where she's going with this.

"Lilah?"

"What? Hmmm? Oh, what I was going to ask was if I hadn't landed on your doorstep in a storm, were you planning to come talk to me, ever? It felt like you were ghosting me and I…" She plucks restlessly at the sheet covering her knees. "I… well, I'd like to know." She bites her lip while raising her eyes to meet mine with a slight hint of challenge in her gaze.

I still her restless fingers by claiming her hands in mine. "Yes, I hadn't worked out the details because the guys showed up early. Are you saying that you missed me?" I lean in to claim her lips too, but she pushes my shoulder back. "Todd, I'm serious."

I sigh and sit back. "Me too. Originally, I'd planned to whisk you away to a fancy dinner in Seattle, but when I realized you didn't associate me with the band, I knew that wouldn't work because someone would have outed me in the first five minutes. Which probably would have gotten awkward quickly. So I was trying to figure out how to sort that out without you thinking it was a big deal to me when the Gazette showed up. Then I knew you'd know sooner than I anticipated, and I had a new problem to solve which was really the same problem in new clothes. How to convince you that I don't give a damn about your taste in music as long as you have a taste for me. Which you seemed okay with earlier today, so can we test that theory out again? Now?" I dive in and rain smacking kisses along the length of her collarbone while her brain turns all that over. I can tell because I can practically hear the wheels cranking, not to mention her sudden inhale followed by a hum that's chased by a small growl.

"You could have told me more about yourself earlier. You've been coming in every day for coffee for months!"

"You'd have gone out with the guy that walked in and announced, 'Hi, I'm famous and have lots of money'?" I ask her skeptically.

"Well, probably not," she acknowledges with a small smile and an eye roll. "But there are a million ways somewhere in the middle to clue me in before I made a fool of myself."

"Sweetheart, I had no idea until then that you didn't know. Most of the island does. A month ago, I would have said all of it, but you can't be the only holdout."

She humphs under her breath before pulling me close. "Still, I think maybe you should apologize properly for making me miss you so badly."

I can sense her defenses softening, so I take advantage by sneaking a kiss. "I agree. What would constitute an adequate expression of my utter and abject regret?" I groan as she wraps her fingers around my swelling cock.

She leans her head back against the pillows with a thoughtful expression while her fingers squeeze lightly. "Hmm. I think I want you to do all the things you would have done if I hadn't literally fallen at your feet. Minus the fancy dinners in the city. I need to get out of your hair and back to my place in the next few days. So prove you mean it and ask me out. Or don't." She lowers her eyes, but the way she's peering at me through her lashes tells me she's actually a little worried that I won't.

"Lilah —"

"What?"

"Can't we do that while you stay here?"

"No. My ankle is getting better. If I take it easy on the stairs and keep walking to a minimum, I'll be fine. I don't want to distract you from your work. And at the same time, I'd like to know you'll put in some effort when you have to walk more than twenty feet to see me. Or not." She smiles slightly, but I can feel the tension in her body.

"Okay. It won't be hard to prove you wrong. Now, do I have to wait for the third date or some other stupid rule or can I fuck you now as the last woman I will ever fuck in my entire life?" Her eyes go round and her lips part. Her hand instinctively tighten on my cock, making me hiss.

"Ooops, sorry! Did I hurt you? Yes, please. Unless I..."

I don't let her finish that sentence. Instead, I soothe my aching cock in the soft comfort of her pussy. Lilah's sweet sigh of surrender is enough to make me forget that she just said she was moving out before she's even moved in.

14

LILAH

I'm astonished at how my world has changed in one long weekend. My ankle is sore and going up and down the stairs at my place will be no picnic, but I'm ready to get back to my own surroundings. I wish I could drag Todd away with me for his own sake. The amenities of being a billionaire aren't lost on me, but when even Todd isn't enjoying them, I don't see them becoming more enticing than they already have. Maybe if he lived some place that truly suited him, I'd find it more appealing. I don't know. Time to go home.

When I woke up this morning, Todd was already out of bed. I presume he's downstairs somewhere. I get dressed as fast as I can manage and pack up my meager bags like I'm in a hotel room and planning to check out. Then I cautiously limp out of the room and make my way to the stairs. I'm not sure where my crutches are, but possibly downstairs, or maybe they never even made it out of the car.

Thankfully, nobody is around as I wince my way down, one stair at a time. It's okay except for the part where I have to put all my weight on the bad leg. That hurts like a bitch. The kitchen shows evidence of breakfast. It's mostly cleaned up, but the scent of bacon still hangs in the air and I breathe it in. I don't need to cook up another mess just for myself. The bread is still on the counter, so I pop a few slices into the toaster and go looking for butter and jam. I wonder if Lance has already headed for the coffee shop? If he hasn't, I can probably convince him to give me a ride down with him. But then I glance at the clock and realize I slept half the morning away. It's nearly 10:00!

I eat my toast standing at the counter in the kitchen, mostly balancing my weight on one leg, and then refill my coffee cup to go exploring — slowly. Within five minutes, I've reached my first conclusion: the house is weird and the views are stupendous. And there are very few signs that Todd actually lives here. The basement area was the most lived in of the rooms I've encountered. There's no dust, so whoever is taking care of it is thorough, but it still has that empty aspect of a house that's not a home.

There's a cheerful knock on the door. When I don't hear any footsteps approaching, I limp towards the front door to open it. There's a gorgeous nearly six foot blonde woman on the other side with her fist raised ready to knock again. Her eyebrows shoot up when she sees me, but she smiles before saying, "Oh, hi. Are you the new housekeeper? I'm Amanda. I believe TK is expecting me."

He is? I don't know quite what to do. "Um, come in. I'm not sure where he is at the moment. Let me just check."

Amanda pays no attention to me, moving past me and into the living room like she's been here many times before. I stare after her, wondering if I should recognize her from TV or something. I don't though. I glance around and spy one of the many house phones. Maybe the guys are down in the studio. Todd said to press the number three, right? I hit the intercom function and the right digit and listen to it beep.

Then I hear Todd's voice, "Baby? Is it important?"

"Um. A woman named Amanda just showed up. Said you were expecting her?" I don't know what I was anticipating in response, but it wasn't a sudden dial tone. I stare down at the phone and then look around for Amanda. She's nowhere to be seen. How very strange.

Less than a minute later Karl comes rushing into the front hall, but like he's trying not to look like he's in a hurry. Quick steps and his slightly clipped speech are what give him away. "There you are, Lilah, sorry to keep you waiting. Todd said he'll pay you for your time at the end of the week. I'll take you home now."

He doesn't look to the right or left, so he can hardly miss my dropped jaw.

"Karl? What the fu —"

He grabs my elbow and propels me in front of him and out the door, completely ignoring my hisses of pain when my ankle protests. He opens the passenger door of the truck and practically pushes me inside. But he takes the time to poke and prod the contents of the back for a solid minute before getting in behind the wheel. He reaches over me to open the glove compartment and snags a set of keys.

Finally, I find words again. "Karl? What's going on?"

He doesn't say a word until he's gunned the engine and cleared the end of the driveway.

"Amanda is Todd's stalker. She got out of prison last week. Nobody thought she'd get here this fast, though."

"But then we need to go back…" I'm frantically trying to undo my seatbelt so I can fling the door open and walk back. Like that would ever work, but Karl flings a mom arm in front of me. "No! You'll make things worse."

I shrink into myself at his harsh words. Karl softens his tone, but only barely. He's still driving like a crazy man. "She's bat-shit crazy, but also really smart. I give her less than two seconds in the same room with you and TK to figure out how you feel about each other. Then she'll want to do more than kill his cat."

"She killed his cat?" I'm screeching in outrage. Not only is that just horrible, but after his childhood, he doesn't deserve to have more things ripped away from him.

Karl glances over at me, confused. "No. He's never had a cat. Think he's allergic, but figuratively. She wants his undivided attention or some such shit. You will just make her more dangerous. Plus, TK would probably do something stupid if he thought you were in danger. Which you would be. So, I'm taking you to the cafe where Lance can lock you up."

"But shouldn't you call the police?"

"I'd be happy to. Thought there weren't any on the island?"

There aren't. "Well, we can call the county sheriff or the state patrol, right?"

"Yeah. We can do that. But I think we have to solve this in the short term on our own."

I don't like this idea of being separated from Todd at all. What if she hurts him? She didn't look that crazy. But then there was that way she just sort of disappeared into the house… I shiver.

TODD

It might not be smart, but Roman and I head deeper into the interior rooms to give Karl a little more time to get Lilah away. Ernie already snuck out the side door to call for reinforcements, even if we all know the chances of them arriving in time to do any good are slim to none. Although if we can manage to incapacitate LuLu, maybe they at least can cart her away.

Roman and I communicate silently with eye contact and hand gestures. We had to do so much of that on stage back when we were touring that it's still second nature. At least something good came out of those years. Mind you, so did Lulu so there's that. I fucking hate the idea of having to live with around the clock security again and making Lilah live like that makes my gut clench painfully.

We take up positions in one of the guest rooms upstairs. It's not ideal, but at least it has some room to maneuver.

And there's not long to wait. "To-od-d!" LuLu calls in a singsong. We started calling her that as a sort of code name in case she was listening outside a window but also as short hand for loony. Because she is that.

"Did you miss me? You didn't write or visit me once while I was in prison. Naughty boy." She drawls that out like she thinks we're lovers playing. My mouth fills with bile at the thought. "Still, you couldn't do better than that fat chick while you waited for me? Or were you worried about making me jealous? In which case, she was a good choice. But I'm back now, so no more girls for you." She bounces into the room like a cheerleader. Except for the raised butcher knife. Ah, fuck.

"Oh, there you are! And Roman too. How lucky can a girl get? I thought you didn't like to share, Todd, but I'm game if you are." She raises her arms in celebration, the knife remaining alarmingly steady. I shift the balance on the balls of my feet, trying to anticipate her next movements. I don't think she even knows — which makes her actions almost impossible to predict.

Feinting left, I extend my right foot. Ignoring my movements, LuLu heads to her left, trips over my foot and sinks the knife straight into Roman's side. The bloom of red on his white shirt is sudden and dramatic. Roman and I are both shocked still, but LuLu isn't. She pulls the knife out and skips out of the room. "Oopsy, gotta run, boys. Todd, baby, stay away from the girls now, you hear?"

My eyes are glued to Roman's side and the welling blood. I grab one of the pillowcases off the bed and press it to his side. Holding it in place, I scan the room for what I'm looking for. There. "Walk with me, Roman. And damn it, hang in there. You die on me, *I'll* haunt *you*." His lips twist, but I can't tell if it's with humor or pain. We sidle over to the dresser and the phone sitting on the top. As soon as I can, I grab it and hit the speed dial for the emergency medical. Everyone on the island pays into a fund for a private helicopter ambulance. And yes, I might make up the difference, but it's not charity so much as saving myself guilt in the future if anything were to happen.

A few short words, and the air ambulance is on the way. Then I dial Karl.

"Lulu under control?" he asks without any preliminaries.

"No. She's on the loose. She stabbed Roman and took off."

He sucks in a breath. "How bad is it?"

"Not good. Helicopter will be here in a few to take him to Seattle. Where's Lilah?"

"She's with Lance in the coffee shop."

"Fuck. LuLu has her in her sights. Get both of them up into the apartment and locked in."

"Surely she's running away rather than make things worse, right?" Karl sounds like he simply doesn't want to believe that LuLu is completely psychotic.

"She's worse than she was. Just do it, man." I hang up as I hear the rotating blades of the ambulance getting closer.

Roman speaks through gritted teeth. "Will you tell Lottie? And if I don't make it, tell her I love her?"

I stare at him and brace my free hand on his back so I can press the sticky fabric harder against his wound. "Are you nuts? First off, you're not allowed to die and second, wouldn't you rather tell her you love her now, while you're alive and can do something about it?"

"Not really. Don't want to scare her off."

I roll my eyes at that one. But I don't have time to set him straight because medics rush the room and push me out of the way. Extra weight isn't allowed on the air ambulance, so as soon as they've got him on the stretcher and down the stairs, I head into the bathroom to wash up.

It's only as I'm watching the pink-tinged water swirl down the drain that I realize I probably shouldn't be alone in a large house, let alone the shower, with a murderous woman on the loose. It may be after the fact, but locking the bedroom door at least gives me some peace while I get dressed and think through how to handle the situation from here. And where the hell is Ernie?

15

LILAH

I'm ready to tear out my hair and scream. Where are the rest of the guys? Why isn't Todd here already? Are they too macho to think a crazy woman can't hurt them? God, I hope not.

I want to pace or maybe throw things, although doing that around so many plate-glass windows is probably not the best idea. Lance is calmly making coffees for the line that extends halfway to the door. I'm shocked by that, but at least it's something positive in an otherwise shitty day. I can't tell yet if it's his new menu or Lance himself that has the line growing. They *are* mostly all middle-aged women, though, so that may be a clue.

The door flies open with a mighty jingle of the brass bell I fastened to it in case I was in the back. My head jerks up with sudden panic, but I relax again when I see it's only Karl. Except Karl isn't calm in the slightest. He makes a signal with his hand to Lance, who nods imperceptibly before turning to address the line. "Sorry ladies, we need to shut down early so no new orders. Come back when we open up again and mention that Karl over there likes redheads and I'll make you something special that's not on the menu for free." There are oohs and ahs before one enterprising woman steps out of the line and walks towards Karl. "I'm a redhead. Natural… all the way down," she croons and Karl glares. I can't tell if it's at the woman or Lance, but either way, he holds the door open.

"Everyone out now. We need to get to practice." More oohs and ahs, but the line quickly dissipates. There are a few holdouts grabbing their drinks, but in seconds, the cafe is clear and Karl is locking the door. Lance is idly wiping down the counter while staring at Karl.

"Both of you, upstairs, now. Lilah, do you need one of us to carry you?"

I shake my head no. His gaze softens. "Then follow me up. I'm going to make sure LuLu's not hiding out already."

"Where's Todd?" I cross my arms over my stomach because suddenly it aches like crazy.

"He's fine. For now. Come on, we'll talk upstairs." He heads through the back like he knows where he's going. I can hear his feet thump on the stairs and then nothing. Lance is making gestures at me so hesitantly I get to my feet while casting glances out at the street. The apartment doesn't have very big windows and they face the alley, so I don't really want to go where I can't see Todd coming. He *is* coming, isn't he?

Lance pushes me in front of him and through sheer crowding like a sheepdog, gets me up the stairs and into the apartment. Karl is waiting for us and not only locks the door behind us but moves the credenza I use for my keys and mail to block the door.

I blink. "What is going on?"

"She stabbed Roman. Todd got him on an air ambulance, but LuLu's gone MIA. We need to stay here until further notice."

"Shouldn't we call him, make sure he's okay?"

"I don't want to distract him. Todd can take care of himself." Karl sounds not quite as confident as I would like about that statement.

"And Roman couldn't? He looked bigger to me." Neither of them can deny it. Although Todd is probably faster on his feet. I sink down on the small loveseat, my stomach now cramping with nerves.

"He'll be safer if he knows you're here and out of danger, Lilah," Karl says softly, stretching out on the couch with a sigh. I can tell his body is still tense and ready to jump though, so I'm suspicious the act is all for me. Like yawning to make me sleepy or some similar form of auto-suggestion.

I would totally be pacing if my ankle were up to it... a burst of inspiration sends me into the kitchen. I think I have — yes, just enough on hand to make a half-pan of brownies. I set everything on the counter and then perch my hip on the edge of a stool so I can concentrate on the magic of butter and chocolate while we wait. I'm all for going off to save Todd, but I don't think these two will let me.

When the oven dings to signal it's finished pre-heating, both Lance and Karl jump slightly. Yep, they're not as relaxed as they're pretending. I greet their covert glances with raised eyebrows before sliding the small pan into the oven. But I freeze when I hear an ominously familiar and too friendly knock on the door. For one thing, that should be impossible because both the shop and the interior lower door were locked behind us. And then there's the fact that I heard the same exact knock only a few hours ago before chaos was unleashed.

I freeze, my eyes wide with panic. Karl must pick up his cue from me because he slides silently to his feet and then over to the window to check the alley. Lance moves to my side and picks up my largest kitchen knife, which isn't that huge, like he's going to protect us both with it. I appreciate the gesture, but I'd probably have better luck throwing eggs at the woman.

"Fuck," Karl curses quietly before moving over to the barricaded door.

"What the hell, man?" Lance mutters as Karl works to open the door.

"She set fire to the place, dude. Let's get Lilah out of here."

I glance helplessly at my oven. A fire? On top of everything? And where is Todd? I can feel tears gathering, but I clamp down on them with an iron will. I'll cry later. Hurriedly, as Karl grabs my elbow, I hit the off button on the oven. What if they put out the fire and then I start a second? That would be the kind of irony that makes up my life.

TODD

There's no sign of LuLu anywhere in my now empty house. That would be a good thing if I had some proof that she was somewhere else less dangerous, but I don't. Silently I wish I'd paid more attention to police procedurals on TV because honestly I don't even know what to look for to see what direction she went. Hell, I don't have a clue if she arrived on foot or by car. Fuck.

I send a quick text message to Ernie and Karl. Just in case either is caught up in something dangerous. Karl had better not be, because then that would mean Lilah was, too. When nobody answers me, I do another perimeter search and come up with no new clues. I'm reasonably positive she's not in the house, but as long as everybody else is out, I honestly don't care. I grab the keys to my secret indulgence, a sleek Japanese motorcycle that can maneuver easily around tight corners. Mostly I take it on long slow rides down the back roads where few people live in the off-season.

Pulling to a halt abruptly at the foot of the hill, I almost burst out laughing despite the seriousness of the situation. Ernie is tied to a tree. Fairly effectively based on how his arms are bound to the trunk. He looks unhurt, so that's something, but the expression on his face... because he doesn't need my help. Another rescuer has beaten me to it. Kristy is on her knees sawing on the ropes, her face just about level with Ernie's umm, well let's just say Ernie seems pretty happy to see her in every way possible except for the burning red of his cheeks. His eyes plead with me to save him from the inevitable embarrassment when Kristy notices his condition.

"Need any help, Kristy?" I call from the side of the road.

"Keep a lookout while I get this idiot free?" she calls without looking up.

"Idiot?" Ernie squawks, looking down at the top of her head with a frown.

"Apologies. Cognitively challenged person of unannounced gender and sexual preference."

I have to bite my cheek to keep from laughing at Ernie's face. He pulls at his arms and the last of the rope loosens and falls free. As she rises to a standing position, Kristy gives Ernie's bulge a friendly pat. "Maybe keep the bondage experiments in the bedroom next time, alrighty?"

His mouth opens and closes a few times while he rubs the feeling back into his arms.

"Kristy, maybe you should stick with us?" I ask cautiously, well aware I can't fit more than one extra person on my bike.

"Naw, I was an MP for two tours. I'm armed and I know how to use it." She pats her left back pocket with confidence as she heads back towards her van.

"You know who we're looking for?"

She gives me a curt nod. "Ernest here filled me in. At least he's observant." Her mouth curves in a slightly wry half smile. Then she checks the back of her van and underneath with clearly practiced precision. Ernie sits down on the rear of the bike with a grimace.

"I don't stand a chance with her, do I?" He sounds wistful, and I have to stare at him for a full minute.

"What did I miss?"

"Not much. LuLu caught me by surprise. Pretty classic, really. She blindfolded me and then tied me up."

I groan. "So you didn't see where she went?"

"No. She was on foot. Then the Valkyrie in a cleaning van showed up." He sighs again like a lovesick comic hero.

"Right. Let's get everyone safe and accounted for before you start making heart eyes."

Even ignoring the speed limits, it's a long five minutes to the village. I head straight for the marina and coffee shop but am stopped dead by the sight of the island's lone, aging firetruck blocking the road, the ladder extended to the back of the coffee shop. Shit.

My heart is in my throat as I stop the bike and jump off, ignoring Ernie's yelp. I search the gathering crowd and start to push people aside to get to the building. That's when I hear Lilah's soft giggle, like my ears are specially tuned to pick her out of a crowd. My eyes track to find her. There. Sitting on an upturned bucket while some punk in a t-shirt fondles her ankle.

16

LILAH

Staring at Mike's dark head as he inspects my ankle for proper rotation and movement has me thinking about another dark head, one that I'm desperately worried about.

"Keep the dancing to a minimum and you'll be fine," Mike pronounces. I laugh with relief and the slightly fantastical image of me dancing anywhere, anytime. Not happening. There's a low growl that has the hairs on my neck standing straight up.

Fierce eyes target me and I glance up, startled. Instinctively, I jump up and practically kick poor Mike in the head as I hurl myself into Todd's arms. "You're here! You're safe." I rain kisses on his face. Eventually, his stern jaw relaxes a smidge.

"Lilah, what happened? Why is that bozo touching you?" he growls in my ear, his arms tightening into steel bands around me. Nothing ever felt so good.

"Who? Oh, you should meet Mike. He's the new EMT for the island. He moved here from California to escape the rat race," I tell him while patting his shoulders and anywhere else I can reach just to make double-sure he's not hurt and didn't get stabbed even a little bit.

"Why do you need an EMT, baby?" his growl is noticeably less growly, but still not what I would describe as normal.

"Hmm? Oh, your stalker girlfriend started a smudge fire in the coffee shop. The guys think it was as a distraction so she could get off the island unseen." I look over his shoulder to locate Karl and Lance, but they've been absorbed into the crowd. It's not a big population, as I've said before, but when the entire village is crammed into one small area of a single street, it's still too many people.

"So you're okay?" He's patting me discretely as well and I can't hold back the smile.

"Yes, I'm totally fine. How's Roman?"

He blinks and then frowns. "I don't know. I haven't had a chance to call and check. Fuck. Someone needs to call Lottie and Sylvie to let them know he's in the hospital."

"I can do it? Or should it be someone they know better?"

"I don't even know what hospital he's in, so it'll have to wait a minute. First priority is making sure LuLu isn't still a threat."

"You can put me down now, you know?" I kiss him once more while I still have the reach and then slide down his lean body.

Todd, of course, continues to frown down at me. "I liked it better when I knew you weren't going to wander off."

I giggle at that one. "Don't you think you should have your hands free, just in case?"

"Only if you promise to stick close. You don't even have a phone on you, do you?" He asks accusingly, like I could really do anything about it when Karl whisked me out of the house without even my bag.

Giving him a small sassy salute, I shake my head and roll my eyes.

Before I can say a word, Todd has me pinned to his side. I've been so worried I don't even mind. I don't want to lose him in the crowd, either. Tentatively, I reach my arm around his waist. It shouldn't be a big thing. A million couples walk around in public like this every day. But I don't or at least I haven't. It's making a public declaration to all of Embrace Island that Todd and I are an item.

I'm expecting every single woman in the crowd to be glaring at me, so I'm a little surprised when I realize that absolutely nobody is paying attention to us. They're all focused on the ladder truck. I giggle to myself, a little embarrassed at my expectations. Todd looks down at me with a quizzical expression.

I shake my head. "I don't know. I think I was expecting people to be shocked to see us together."

"Do you want them to be shocked?" His lips quirk with humor and I sigh softly.

"Not really. It's just, um… I imagined this for a long time like something that was unrealistic, more of a pure fantasy, you know?"

I need him to understand — to get that I'm not looking to soak up any residual fame. Then I straighten my spine. "But that doesn't mean you're completely off the hook. I don't want you to think I'm easy. I still want that proper date."

Todd's back to frowning. "About that, Lilah. I…"

He doesn't get a chance to finish his sentence as one of the firemen comes up to me. "The fire's out, but it's not safe for anyone to sleep in there until the smoke's cleared. Understand?"

I nod despondently. Another rug ripped out from under me. But it's minor compared to Roman's injuries or having Todd back in one piece.

Just then Todd's pocket starts vibrating. He answers it absently, his eyes still tracking my smallest movement. Then he stops in his tracks. "Lottie? What do you mean? You're coming here?"

I can hear the frantic tone in the woman's voice, even with the phone held against Todd's cheek. "No, of course you're welcome. So is Sylvie…"

Todd grimaces and I try to piece together the bits I've heard. His gaze leaves me and lands on Lance. Oh. That not-so-secret feud, or what I secretly think is repressed sexual tension, but none of the guys, particularly Roman and Lance, want to hear that theory from me.

"Just be careful, okay? One of us will pick you up from the ferry. Don't worry about it, but watch your back."

He hangs up with a sigh and slides his phone back into his pocket. "As I was saying. Can we date while you live in my house? I'm not going to be able to sleep unless I know you're safe."

I chew on that for a minute. Same goes really. As much as I want to make sure I'm not imposing myself on his easy-going nature, I'm worried about him. Amanda is one crazy bitch.

"Okay, but I don't think your house is safe either. Can we stay someplace else? Somewhere your LuLu hasn't already scoped out and planted cameras?"

TODD

When did Lilah get so cynical? She's not wrong. I doubt LuLu had a chance to plant anything, but I didn't think she'd just sail in and stab Roman either and look how that turned out.

"What about the other guys?" She looks around, presumably for Karl, Ernie, and Lance. The three stooges are busy posing for tourist selfies.

"They're grown-ups. But if it makes you feel better, I'll send them over to Uncle Lou's. They can pitch a tent in his backyard for all I care."

"And Roman?" she asks quietly.

"Out of surgery, according to Lottie. He called her and Sylvie to tell them to come here so LuLu doesn't try to track them down. A week ago I'd have said she wasn't that crazy, but now I'm not sure she has any limits. Lottie wanted to meet him at the hospital but he said if he found her there, he'd put her on a two month no-port cruise all on her own."

"Is there such a thing?" Lilah looks doubtful, but I grin.

"If there isn't, he'd charter one. They both stare at each other whenever the other one isn't looking. She'll come straight here because he made his point about how worried he'd be if she goes to the hospital."

"Come on, let's go figure out where we're sleeping tonight." I tug her gently to the edge of the crowd. "At least while I get some security experts in, we can stay on the boat? But I don't want it in the marina, so we'll have to find some other place to moor it temporarily."

"You have a boat, too?" Her eyes go round and I hope the damn yacht isn't another nail in my coffin.

"I keep thinking about selling it but haven't gotten around to it."

"You're wealthier than I think, aren't you?"

How the hell do I answer that question? "I'm deprived in other ways. Nobody's kissed me in... God, at least twelve hours."

"You poor thing." It's good that she's smiling, but unfortunate that she's not making any kind of move to rectify the situation. "Tell me more about this boat. Does it have a bathroom?"

"Yes." Three actually, but I don't want to scare her off the idea.

"And some way to make coffee in the morning?"

"Yes, and breakfast." I'm wracking my brain trying to think of who has a dock where I could tie Bianca up and trust that Lilah would be safe.

"There's a dock near my friend Bethany's place. Do you think that would work?"

"Maybe. I'll have to check the depth. Ever been on a motorcycle?"

She shakes her head, looking nervous but not outright refusing.

"I have some expectations, if we're going to be living together so soon," she announces flatly as we reach the edge of the crowd where I abandoned the bike.

"Okaaay." I wait, curious to see what she's come up with besides going on proper dates.

"You work on the album stuff every day. No excuses."

"And?" What the hell is she leading up to?

"And… I want an hour of conversation and an hour of sex every single damn day. I don't care when or in what order." She flicks a nervous glance my way, as if she's scared about how I'm going to react to that.

I'm grinning with delight. That's how I react. How did I get so lucky to have her land on the same small island as me? "Done. Is that the minimum or the maximum?"

"Minimum. You want to talk into the night that's on you, but you still have to do the music the next day."

"Fine by me. Anything else?"

She bites her lip for a minute. "A hug every now and then wouldn't go amiss. And when it's time, I'm going to want to hear your plans for the future. Concrete ones involving everything from the house to the band. But I'm not ready to discuss that just yet."

"Fair enough. Can I ask what prompted the hour of sex? I'm not complaining, but I didn't see that one coming."

Her lips twitch, but her voice is steady when she finally speaks. "You hold back a lot. I think it's because you know you reveal more than you want to when you're not in complete control. I want that from you — that level of honesty. And I also want to be fucked. I've had a lot of time to imagine sleeping with you and twice was not enough."

She reaches over without looking at me and pats my ass like she's trying to be patronizing. She's too adorable to pull it off, though, so I grab her hand and place it over my aching cock. We're partially obscured by the bike, so it's not quite the blatant PDA she'd be uncomfortable with. Her little hitch of breath and tiny squeak immediately give her innocence away, though. She's putting up a brave front, but she's quaking deep inside. I let her hand go, but not before raising it to my lips for a kiss in the center of her palm.

17

LILAH

I'm exhausted. It's been a hell of an emotional rollercoaster day and it's not over yet. I don't actually have a bed for the night to fall into. But I've got the hot guy of my dreams right here earnestly promising me steamy sex on a daily basis. This has to be a dream. Discretely, I pinch myself and then wince. I'm not sure that proved anything, really.

When we pull up in front of Bethany's cute cottage, I look for clues that she's home and don't see any. Maybe soon? I guess we can go look at the dock, though, in the meantime. I don't think it's even technically on her property, but the place next door has been empty for years, according to her. Certainly since I've been on the island and the small stone cottage has that air of neglected beauty. Like it was once well-loved and that energy still persists despite the tall weeds in the front yard.

Todd heads down towards the water with that loping stride that always catches my attention.

Even from back here, I can see his frown when he looks down at the dilapidated dock. It's still standing though, and as long as you're careful where you put your feet, it's safe enough. I think.

He picks a path down the length of it and then peers over the edge before looking back at me and shaking his head slightly. Uh oh. I walk down to meet him at the shoreline as he heads back.

"No good?" I ask anxiously. I wanted this to work. I've had enough stress for the day.

"I doubt you could get anything bigger than a single seater sailboat in there. The depth is maybe six feet. Bianca would be a beached whale."

"Bianca is your boat?"

His lips twitch. "Yes, and before you ask, she wasn't named after a woman, not exactly. She was named after my uncle's dog."

"So now what?"

"How about I take you to the marina and the boat for the night? We'll pull out into the harbor and then figure something else out tomorrow."

I blink at him. "That would be nice. Too bad that little place isn't yours too." I nod at the cottage on the shore behind us.

Todd studies it over my shoulder. "Nobody lives there?"

I shake my head. "Bethany says not as long as she's lived here, which is over ten years. I think there was an old lady there and then her family moved her to the mainland when she needed more care. Not sure who owns it now. Nobody seems to come."

"Hmm. Just a sec. I'm going to go peer in the windows." And off he goes to do exactly that. It doesn't take long to circumnavigate the small house. It looks like it's not more than four rooms in total, including the upstairs.

Todd looks thoughtful when he jogs back down the hill. "Okay, ready to relax on the boat?"

I nod almost desperately. I want to put my brain on hold for the next twenty-four hours and not have to think about anything.

Todd stops off at the small grocery and I opt to stay on the bike, mostly because I don't want to be asked to make any decisions inside. I told him to buy wine. Anything else is extra even though I know what he has in his mansion cellar is far superior to anything offered by the place advertising fish sticks at two for one. There are enough people around that I should be safe enough but that doesn't stop Todd's frown of concern as he reluctantly heads inside on his own. I'll bet he's never shopped so fast in his life.

The island's marina is bigger than you might expect. Some developer half a century ago thought he'd bring in the big tourists in a build-it-and-they-will-come mentality. It sort of worked?

Every summer a handful of die-hard boaters show up and buy gas and supplies. But they don't linger. And most of them don't even buy coffee! So the slips are almost all empty, but we still have to park on the main street and walk quite a distance past those unmet grandiose plans to arrive at Todd's spot. I'm dying of curiosity because this must be where he's been going every time I see him go by the shop.

Oops, that reminds me I didn't even glance at the Embraceable Brew on the way by. Todd catches me looking down the street. "Your shop is fine."

I'm struck silent though by the hulking, shiny white stretch of fiberglass taking up my entire field of vision when we finally stop at the end of the dock. *Bianca* is written on the side in flowing navy blue script. There's no doubt this is Todd's 'boat'.

"Todd," I say ominously when I can finally speak again.

"It's not as big as it looks. Come see inside." He tugs me towards the silver ladder affixed to the side. You have to climb a *ladder* to get onto his damn boat.

"Todd, this isn't a boat. It's a yacht."

"It floats, therefore it's a boat."

He picks me up by the waist and sort of suspends me on the ladder like someone hanging a painting on the wall while blindly feeling for the hook. I sigh and start climbing. I might as well see the rest of the billionaire lifestyle.

TODD

Well, that actually went a little better than I expected. Taking the groceries down to the small galley kitchen, I let Lilah go exploring without me. When I hear her choked gasp, I try to imagine what in particular brought that reaction. Before long, my curiosity is killing me and I go in search of her.

I find her frozen in the doorway to the main state room. I never bothered redecorating and I've never used that one, so I'd forgotten. "You can sleep in there if you'd like. There are sheets and blankets in the cupboard."

She turns to eye me with wonder. "You don't sleep here?"

I shrug uncomfortably. "Can you believe I find these rooms claustrophobic? I haven't slept on the boat in years and when I did, it was almost always in the main cabin. Higher ceilings and more windows."

Without a word, she turns into my arms and gives me a solid hug, her face buried in my chest. We stand like that for a moment. Then I brush my hand over her back awkwardly. "Lilah? What's the matter, baby?"

She squeezes her arms tight before lifting her head. "I think I finally understand why the money is an afterthought for you. Let's camp out in the main cabin. I don't want to be in here without you." And with that, she pushes past me and back down the corridor, turning her back on the gilded bed inlaid with mother-of-pearl. It's a bit ostentatious, but lovely. It's a bed fit for a mermaid princess. I stare after my girl, who says she'd rather curl up in blankets on the floor for my sake.

Detouring by the galley, I pour her a glass of wine and go in search of her again. The boat isn't that big. This time I find her out on the upper covered deck, closing her eyes into the light wind. She turns and takes the glass from me without a word.

Several sips later, she announces, "God, I needed that. It's been a helluva day."

I wince. "Come on, let's sit down over here and I'll start convincing you it was all a bad dream."

She smiles a little wistfully but follows me over to the built-in seating that's tucked into the curve so it has some wind protection. The cushions have seen better days, but they're dry and functional. I slide in behind her so she can rest her head on my chest and still sip her wine in comfort. I needed this, maybe as much as Lilah did. But this isn't about me, not now.

She stares out at the marina, dead quiet in the afternoon sunshine. Not a soul coming or going, the only movement is the gentle bobbing of the weekend pleasure craft.

"Why do you live with so many things you don't like?" she finally asks with a stilted hesitancy like she's pushing too far too fast.

"Like what?"

"Like this yacht that you're not comfortable in, like that house that you say you hate at least once a day."

"It's mostly penance for youthful folly and a pinch of lack of inspiration as to what to replace it with. The house was something I paid way too much for in an attempt to give to my uncle to show my appreciation, but was really more about me showing off. Which is why he turned it down. That and he's smart enough to know what won't suit him. But I have to live somewhere and I do want to stay close to him if I can to at least keep him supplied with 'damn fool' technology, like phones and hearing aids."

Lilah rubs her free hand gently over my arm, where it's wrapped around her midsection. "Does it bother you that people resist you trying to help?"

Denial is on the tip of my tongue, but I bite it back to give her the respect of a thoughtful answer. "I'd like to feel like I'm your first choice and that you understand that's the way I feel about you," I finally say quietly. "That, and I'm naturally grumpy," I add cheerfully, trying to lighten the mood.

Lilah snorts and thumps my thigh lightly with her fist. "Idiot."

Since she says it like a damn caress, she can call me that all day long.

LILAH

Todd isn't one of those obviously sensitive guys. I mean, he's not brash, but he always has it so together that I don't want to spoil this moment by saying the wrong thing, which I do seem to have a talent for. Instead, I bust my brain trying to think of a way to show him that it's not the lack of eligible bachelors on the island that has me drooling over him. We could be in the middle of New York and he'd still be the one to catch my eye. And I'm pretty sure all the other female eyes for a six-block radius. Maybe we should avoid visiting crowded cities on principle.

I've also figured out that action is clearly Todd's love language. From the secret tips to carrying me around, he's all about demonstrating his feelings. So I need to *do* something to make it clear to him how important he is to me.

He leans over briefly and refills my glass. I snuggle back against him. "This is nice, you know? Just sitting and talking. We haven't really done that, not calmly anyway." I amend wryly, thinking of my midnight crying jag.

Todd doesn't say anything in response, just sweeps my hair off my neck before pressing an open mouth kiss to that nobbly bit at the base of my neck. My belly tightens and I turn my head to peer back at him sideways. "You going to follow up on that, mister?"

His eyes soften. "Later. Right now you're relaxing." He says it like an order which makes me smile.

But I'm not going to let go until I say what's on my mind. "Todd? You could have been the one stabbed today. I'm not saying I'm glad it was Roman, but someone could have died — all because you insisted on being a hero."

Todd rests his chin on the top of my head. "I'd do it again if it meant you staying safe, but I didn't factor in you not having a phone with you. Clearly, I was an idiot and I'll let you plan the next deranged stalker escape, I promise. Also, I'll need you to practice telling me off. You lacked confidence, just now."

I can't turn my head because he has it pinned with his chin. But I want to — if only to sputter at him.

He tickles my side lightly. "Try it now, baby. Repeat after me. Todd, you're being an idiot."

"How is doing what you tell me, telling you off?" I scoff with mock outrage.

"You can ad lib the next time."

"Fine. Todd, you are being an absolute idiot."

He pinches my side lightly, probably for adding the adjective. "See? That wasn't so hard. When you're least expecting it, I'll give you some opportunities to practice spontaneously."

I mull that over, then I sit up so I can look him in the eyes. They're twinkling madly and I can tell he's biting his cheek not to smile.

"Did you just give yourself a free pass for fucking up?"

His shrug is overly casual, and my eyes narrow in suspicion. He knows he's not fooling me, but I don't think that's really what he's trying to say here.

I twist so I can kiss his chin lightly. "You'll always be *my* idiot, Todd. Now why don't you show me how much you really missed me?"

He quirks an eyebrow. "Really? In broad daylight? You hussy."

I roll my eyes. "What have you been reading? And I didn't mean out here on the deck. There may not be people around, but those seagulls are way too interested in what we're doing."

Todd snorts and then tugs me up. "I think maybe I should feed you first."

I make a face again behind his back. Did I say I wanted him going all alpha and in charge on me? I take it back.

"Maybe I'll just go get started without you then," I say sassily and make like I'm going to move past him and down into the main lounge.

He growls and wraps a long arm around my waist, tugging me back. "Not unless I get to watch. And I'd rather you let me do the work this time. Which is why you need to eat. It could be a very long night."

I swallow hard, my mouth suddenly dry. I know he's been holding back the few times we've been together. "What exactly do you have planned?"

He flicks my nose with his finger. "That's for me to know and you to find out — later." And with a wicked leer he turns into the high-end galley and opens up the space-age refrigerator.

18

TODD

I'm distracted from the mundane chore of chopping vegetables by the way Lilah's eyes keep drifting shut. She's precious beyond belief and I can't breathe thinking about how close I came to losing her. Then her head jerks a little, telling me she's ready to fall asleep. She's still curled up on the deck, but I can watch her through the large windows at the front of the lounge. Despite my dirty talk, she needs sleep more than sex right now.

Then I remember the promise she so easily extracted from me. I can't break it on the first day. Hell, I never want to let her down. I add peanut oil to the already hot sauté pan and toss in the sliced but still frozen chicken, stirring it a few times before adding the vegetables I picked up at the small grocery store. Watching Lilah jerk awake again, I don't even care. This time, she sits up straight and scrubs her eyes before turning to meet my gaze. She smiles hesitantly.

Tossing the contents of the pan into two shallow bowls, I carry them out to her.

"That looks good." Lilah smiles again, taking the bowl and the fork I hand to her.

"Hopefully, it's at least edible. After dinner, I'll pull the boat out of the marina, so anybody wanting to get on board will have to swim."

"Or have another boat?" she asks with a smirk and an arched eyebrow.

I nod in concession. "The ladder is detachable. They'll need grappling hooks, too."

She giggles making me glad our adventures are closer to turning humorous. It's going to take a while longer, though, to truly get over that hump, particularly with Roman temporarily out of commission.

"Hey, Todd?" Lilah catches my attention with her anxious whisper.

"Baby? What the matter?"

"I still feel guilty for letting Amanda in. Or LuLu or whatever her name is. I should have known better."

I shake my head at her. "Nonsense. If you'd resisted, she might have gotten violent with you or started a fire or worse. And when they do finally catch her since she did hurt someone, this time they'll lock her up for longer."

Lilah gives a shuddering breath. "So, do you have other stalkers? Anyone else I need to know about?"

I wave my hand dismissively. "One or two. Most of them faded away when we stopped touring. Yet another sign it was the right decision. The few that still send notes and, uh, gifts don't meet the criteria for dangerous, according to my lawyer, anyway."

She bites her lip with concern. "Won't the recent publicity draw them here, though?"

"Maybe. But that's why I put in a call to Alpha Corps. I have a connection that put me in touch with the right people. They've always concentrated on government contracting, but they're looking at getting into private security. A team will be arriving tomorrow."

"Bodyguards?" she squeaks, like I announced we were setting up pole dancers in the living room.

"Not exactly. They're going to work on securing the entire island. Setting up cameras, monitoring the ways in and the ways out. They won't be following you or me from room to room."

Her shoulders relax a little. Then she giggles.

"What?" I ask nervously.

"Your Uncle Lou is going to have a fit."

I roll my eyes. "I'm not going to tell him. Let's see how long it takes him to figure it out."

Taking her empty bowl, I jerk my head towards the interior. "Why don't you get settled and maybe take a nap while I move us out to open water?"

"Don't you need help for that?"

"Nope. Got everything rigged with automation for a solo sailor. It helps that this berth is near the entrance, so pretty much just have to back up."

"Okay. Sheets and blankets?"

"Try the closet at the foot of the stairs. Should be plenty to choose from. But watch your balance on the steps. Don't carry so much that you can't hold on to the railing."

She rolls her eyes more dramatically this time. "Yes, sir." Then she pauses. "Are you always going to be this overprotective?"

I lean down to get my eyes as close to hers as possible, our noses just touching. "Yes." Then I kiss her to truly express why she matters so much. Her lips part, inviting me in, but I pull back. "Stop tempting me, sweetness. We've got work to do."

She huffs lightly but there's a smile brightening her face as she heads towards the short staircase leading below deck.

LILAH

It doesn't take long to build a cozy nest in the main lounge. Like a grown-up blanket fort, I can't wait to curl up and see if I can see stars through the big windows. Even though I know Todd is keeping the yacht moving extra slow, I do have to reach out to brace myself and get my balance as the boat moves through the water. We don't go far though, and it's not long before I can feel the thunk of the anchor tethering us in place.

God, I still can't believe Todd owns a yacht. It seems so out of character. I could see him with a high-end speed boat or one of those tricked-out deep sea fishing things. But this? I pat the wall. "Bianca, we're going to find you someone that truly appreciates you," I promise her. Naturally, that's when I turn around to see Todd leaning against the doorway with his arms folded and a wicked smirk on his face.

I blush. Am I being too forward in giving away his possessions? He stalks towards me.

"Sorry," I mutter.

He looks startled. "For what?"

"Telling your yacht I was going to find her a new owner." It's silly, but still.

Todd grins. "Good. You're in charge of that then, and buying the more sensible replacement. I'll solve the housing issue."

I gape at him, but his expression has gone more serious. He takes my hands and tugs me towards the bed I've arranged on the floor. "Lilah? Tell me what you want here, tonight. I promised to fuck you and you should know I'm always up for that, but you seem exhausted. So I need to know…" his words trail off as he eyes me with concern. That does it for me, right there. I flow into his arms, snuggling my nose into his firm chest.

"I want slow and easy. I want you filling me up so that those scary empty spots are gone completely."

With only a sweet kiss on the top of my head, he acquiesces and leads me over to the makeshift bed. We don't speak as he undresses me and then simply flows over me. His kisses are like a soft spring rain — refreshing — and make me smile.

When he enters me, I swear his cock is even bigger than before, but I'm ready for him. My channel is slick with need. Instead of pounding into me (which normally I wouldn't mind in the slightest) he just keeps pushing deeper and further. Everything in me is throbbing in rhythm with the gently gathering pressure, like the entire ocean is holding back, waiting to flood my pussy. Then Todd sucks gently on my earlobe and I explode in a quick succession of seismic waves.

That sets Todd off. Still without speaking, I stare into his eyes, maybe even into his soul, as he cums with deep, long pulses. I smile with love, with satisfaction, and the sheer joy of giving. Because he needed this, maybe even more than I did.

When I can feel his heart rate return to something resembling normal, I reach up and kiss his jaw. "I think we should get married next weekend." I try to say it calmly, like I'm suggesting vacuuming out the car, but I can't restrain my giggles when his eyes widen and his breath catches.

"What happened to taking a step back and just dating? Not that I'm complaining. Simply trying to keep up."

"I already know everything I need to know about you." I wave a dismissive hand, delighted that I've managed to surprise him.

"Oh, really?"

I pout as he pulls out of me so he can flip us over. Sprawled on his chest, he pulls me up far enough to kiss me. "So while I have you in this agreeable mood, let me just confirm — we're going to tie the knot next weekend, no prenup, and we're living together from here on out."

I frown a little at his lack of financial responsibility, but then I force myself to relax. "Yes. If you want to be crazy with your money, I'm not going to stop you. Much. And besides, I'm never going to let you go and I don't want you ever thinking I'm only sticking around for your money. So I'm going to help you give it away."

Todd grins. "That's the spirit. Now go to sleep or I'll have to fuck you again out of sheer relief."

I curl into him with a smile. "In the morning. Love you."

He lets out this huge exaggerated sigh. "Did you have to say that first again, too? Now it's just anticlimactic if I say it back."

I lift my head so I can see his face. He's pouting, but his eyes are twinkling. I roll my eyes and put my head back on his chest. "Write a bad song about it."

His laughter rolls like a wave under my cheek, and I close my eyes, smiling.

TODD

Waking up in a nest of blankets with Lilah curled up against me, her cheek resting on my chest, is the sweetest thing ever. And I would gladly stay here all day, but I've got phone calls to make to ensure this moment keeps happening over and over again. *Maybe in a bed next time* I amend as my back protests my instructions to bend and stand.

It's a cold, wet, and windy day outside, pretty

typical for November, but even the fanciest boat isn't as well insulated as a house, certainly not on the decks that have doors to the outside. The waves are a bit choppy so we're rocking a bit, but Lilah doesn't seem to be disturbed by it. I head into the galley to start coffee and find my phone.

I'm not going to say money doesn't make life easier because it definitely does. It pays for the lawyer I can delegate making a purchase to before breakfast and the judge that finally consents to make the trip out to the island to marry us next weekend. Not that I'm saying he was bought exactly, but he seemed a lot more agreeable after I told him he could bring his wife and daughter and yes, the entire band would be present. I didn't mention Roman, partly I'm afraid to jinx his recovery, but we also don't need any leaks that might inflame LuLu or her fellow stalkers.

Jason, the lawyer, gets back to me within the hour, just as Lilah starts stirring. "It's yours. There's a key under the flowerpot by the back door and I'll have paperwork ready for your signature by lunch. After this, though, I'm going to start charging you double for answering the phone before ten."

"Okay." I can feel his surprise over the phone line, but my attention is all on the woman sitting up. The naked woman with generous unbound breasts and a sleepy smile. I hang up on Jason before he can start asking annoying questions.

"Ready for coffee?" I call to Lilah softly.

"Hmm? Uh, sure, but after I brush my teeth. Is there a robe around here or something?"

"Nobody can see you except me." Call me crazy, but why cover up such bounty?

"Maybe not, but I'm freezing." She crosses her arms over those breasts I was admiring and shivers.

Can't have that. Frowning with regret, I pull an oversized fleece hoodie out of a storage bench and toss it to her. "We could sail to the Caribbean?"

"Someday, it would be kind of a long trip from this side of the continent." She pulls the navy fleece over her head and then stands, her legs wide to get her balance as the boat moves against the choppy water. I decide that maybe half-dressed is a good look on her, the dark vee between her legs just a tantalizing hint when she moves.

"New rule. No sex before coffee, so get that look out of your eye." She glares at me, then grins, and moves down the hall to the head.

When she comes back, she saunters over to me and pulls my head down with both hands. She drops a kiss on my jaw, reminding me I haven't had time to shave. I'm not even entirely sure there's a razor onboard. Before Lilah can escape, I capture her mouth for a proper good morning.

"Coffee," she says breathlessly when she pulls back. I hand her the mug I had waiting for her.

"You were up early," she mentions casually after several sips.

"Phone calls to make, and I didn't want to disturb you. We have things to talk about."

"Well, that sounds ominous," she says dryly, and I shake my head.

"Nope, but come here. It's been hours." I tug her over to the bench seat and down on my lap. I swear she rolls her eyes the entire time.

When she's settled comfortably in my arms with her coffee, I catch her up. "A judge is coming out next Saturday to perform the wedding ceremony. Do what you need or want to do in that time frame, but don't plan on leaving the island. It's not safe. I'll give you my credit card so you can go to town online."

"I don't need anything fancy," she says quietly.

I shrug. "Didn't say it had to make the New York Times list. But this will be it for both of us, and besides, we owe it to the island for not announcing everything at the hardware store first."

She looks stricken at that. "Oh my God, you're right. Clem's never going to forgive you."

"That's alright. I'll tell him you're the one that proposed."

She gapes at me and then bursts into giggles. "I want to be there to see his face when you tell him that."

I kiss her instead. "And the other thing is you now own the house next to your friend."

"I do? When did I buy that?" Her eyebrows are getting a workout this morning.

"While you were asleep. You just need to decide if you want to move in and clean and paint or clean and paint and then move in."

"Are you coming with me?"

"What do you think?" I pretend to glare at her.

"I think you're the best rock star ever, but I want to see you bare-chested with a paintbrush. Now *that's* sexy." She grins like she knows she can get me to do anything she wants. She's right. "Can we stay on the boat while we tidy it up?"

"Not without using the dinghy, which could get old quickly."

"Then can we go see inside it now?"

19

LILAH

Sometimes even gazillionaire rock stars need rescuing. So that's what I'm doing, and it's not entirely selfless. Todd needs saving from that house and all the things he dislikes, but can't bring himself to part with. And I need to see him happy, or at least less grumpy.

Convincing him to swing by the new old house to take a look around inside isn't particularly difficult. I know he needs to check on his friends and the current whereabouts of LuLu, but half an hour won't make that much of a difference. I hope.

We find the key not exactly where it was described, but close. It was under the boot scraper, not a flowerpot, but I let that go once Todd has it turning in the lock and we can finally get inside. The place is musty, but you can still feel the love that once flowed here. The wallpaper in the living room is faded but not peeling. Once it had delicate bouquets of violets and butterflies. A little too Victorian for my taste, but

I'll bet it was lovely and perfect for the woman who lived here.

Upstairs, the bedrooms are all well-proportioned with slanted ceilings and old-fashioned light fixtures. It's undeniably sweet. And it needs a lot of work. I look out the window of the back bedroom to the hillside that would have even more sweeping views of the ocean.

Todd comes up behind me and engulfs me, resting his chin on the top of my head.

"Todd, how many millions do you have left?"

He chuckles like I've said something funny. "Plenty. Why?"

I point out the window. "Don't get me wrong, this place is cute and once we fix it up, it'll be a perfect guest house but that... there could be magnificent."

He hums against my back. "You're right. It would be. I've had my eye on this really amazing architect who does basically organic forms in very high tech. But he's not only expensive but reclusive. He doesn't take many jobs and the ones he does take are mostly commercial."

"Have you asked?"

"Nooo. But I can. I've met him. At some charity thing or other a few years back."

"Not that I don't trust you, but show me some

pictures before you contact him? Just so I can see if we're on the same page?"

I can feel Todd slide his phone out of his pocket and then he holds it in front of both of us while he finds what he's looking for.

"There. That's what I'm talking about, but perhaps something a little smaller," he says dryly.

I look at the most gorgeous skyscraper I've ever seen. It's elegant and functional and I just want to reach out and slide my hand over it. I've seen something similar on the news once. "That's William Zver, right? You've *met* him?"

"Once."

"And you can afford to hire him?" I squeak. William Zver is in the caliber that designs country houses for royalty and gets his buildings on the front covers of design magazines. But then, in a way, I guess Todd is in that class of wealth. I just keep forgetting it.

Todd raises his eyebrows. "Probably? It's not like he hands out a price sheet when you shake his hand."

I giggle. "Well, it can't hurt to ask, right? I agree on the style in any event, although more domestic, obviously."

"Seen enough of this place for today?"

I nod. "Yep. There's enough work here. I think we should just bring in a team of contractors. Strip everything back, then paint the walls and re-varnish the floors. It'll be faster than trying to do it ourselves and you need to be in the studio, anyway."

Todd gives me a quizzical look, followed by a slow grin. "Love you, Lilah."

I blink and then blush. "Was I being too bossy?"

"You were being you, and that's exactly what I want."

Rolling my eyes, I let him tug me out of the bedroom and down the stairs. I'm envious of his ability to be so diplomatic with words. Maybe after ten years or so, some of that will rub off on me? A girl can hope.

We're still traveling via Todd's bike, so we can't really chat on our way back to his ugly house. When we pull up, there's a strange car in the driveway and two women standing in front of the door. One has long, dark hair and looks considerably younger than the curvy woman with auburn hair standing next to her.

With a firm press of his hand on my shoulder, Todd makes it clear he wants me to stay where I am. I hesitate. They don't look dangerous, but then neither did Amanda, aka LuLu. Todd takes off his helmet and clears his throat. The women turn. Todd's face lights up. "Lottie? You came together? Did I miss your call?"

The older woman shakes her head and smiles. "No, I picked Vivi up on the way. I thought it might be safer that way, and I wanted my car, seeing as I don't know the island." When Todd leans in and kisses both of them on the cheek, I decide I can get off the bike and stop being the outsider. I'm not entirely sure he hasn't forgotten I'm even here.

The younger woman notices me first and regards me with serious and cautious green eyes. She looks vaguely familiar. Maybe she's a model or someone I'm supposed to recognize. Mind you, I thought that about Amanda slash LuLu too…

Todd turns, but he doesn't startle, so maybe he didn't forget me completely. "Lilah, this is Sylvie, Roman's daughter, and this is Lottie. She's Roman's uh…"

Lottie takes pity on him with a soft smile. "Technically his housekeeper, but I hope I'm more of a friend at this point. I'm certainly worried about him."

Todd nods and then continues the introductions. "Ladies, this is Lilah. You're just in time for the wedding. We're getting married next weekend."

Both women look shocked and then a slow, wicked smile spreads across Sylvie's face and I can finally see the similarity with Roman.

TODD

My life is getting crowded. Don't get me wrong, I want Sylvie and Lottie safe and they'll be good company for Lilah when I have to be somewhere else, but right now I want my now fiancée all to myself. I check my phone impatiently for any messages. It's not safe to wander through the house until it's been cleared.

The sound of a deep growly motor has us all turning nervously to watch the driveway. A dark green truck approaches and two military types get out. They're not in uniform, but they move like they are.

"Mr. Kipling?" One of them calls before giving polite nods to the women. "We're with Alpha Corps. I'm Jed, this is Parker." He jerks his head in the direction of his partner.

"Glad you could make it. How do you want to do this?"

"Let us go in first, please. Y'all wait right where you are. Shouldn't take too long."

The door never did get locked yesterday, so I push it open and gesture for them to enter. Immediately, they go into professional mode, and we can't even hear them moving through the building.

This is the part I hate about having personal security. It's not just the invasion of privacy, it's being pushed to the side as the 'asset', instead of being part of the action. Then I look down at Lilah, biting her lip with concern and let all that go. If I was in there playing cops and robbers, she's be here defenseless. Sort of. Pretty sure LuLu's the one that needs to be worried if she ever encounters Lilah again.

It's a long ten minutes, but finally Jed appears again with a calm face. "Just one more thing, Mr. Kipling. There's a locked room downstairs that we still need to check. Do you want to come with us or…"

I grin when I see the way Lilah's blushing, but I lose it fast when a look of awareness flashes over Jed's face.

"It's just an office. The code is 50702," I growl.

Lilah pokes me in the side, but I'm beyond confused as to what she's worried about.

"You shouldn't give out your code like that," she hisses. So damn adorable.

"I can change it later. I don't want to leave you here out in the open," I answer her, sliding my hands into my pockets.

An eye roll is all I get in appreciation.

Then the rest of the guys pull up in various borrowed vehicles. Not sure where they found them, really. Naturally, Lance keeps a healthy twenty foot radius between him and Sylvie at all times, but based on Lilah's comments from a few days ago, I watch more carefully. They're both eyeing each other when they think the other one isn't looking. And they both have matching expressions like someone kicked their dog. Huh.

"So when's Roman coming back?" someone pipes up, asking what we're all wondering. I feel guilty for not checking up on him in the hospital, but once I knew he wasn't going to die, I figured he was safe where he was.

Lottie answers quietly, "He wants to get here tomorrow, but the hospital won't release him to travel unless it's a licensed ambulance service, so he's trying to find one that will come out to the island."

"Won't he need a nurse or something if he's too banged up to travel?" Karl asks with concern but sounding almost angry.

Lottie flushes slightly, but then straightens her spine. "I am a nurse. I've kept up my license even though I haven't been working in that capacity for a few years."

Pretty much everyone's eyeballs are firing questions at her, but the way she turns away and hunches her shoulders says it's off limits.

"It's all clear — you guys can head in, but until we get cameras in place, please stay inside for the night. We're going to check the perimeter now and clear the garage, then we'll do routine sweeps until morning." Jed jerks everyone's attention away from Lottie. There's something of a communal sigh of relief and then the guys grab the suitcases from Lottie's car. Lance hangs back and then finally clears his throat. "If it's all right with you, Lilah, I'll stay at your place. That way, I can open up in the morning." He studiously doesn't make eye contact with Sylvie, who's looking like someone slapped her.

Lilah, on the other hand, looks worried. "But the smoke… and what if she comes back?"

"We cleaned everything up. The smell will dissipate in a few days. And we put new high-end locks on the doors. Besides, the general consensus is that she's mostly likely already left the island. I'll be fine." He gives her a little grin that has my jaw clenching. I'm not exactly jealous of Lance, but I know how easy it is to fall for Lilah and I'd rather stop that before it starts.

20

TODD

I'm mulling over a happier problem as the guys (minus Lance, who's being an ass) and I prep dinner while the ladies relax in the lounge with periodic glances our way, followed by giggles. I try not to think about the fact that Lilah and Sylvie are about the same age. But Lottie is at least twelve years older and yet you'd never know the three of them haven't been besties for the last decade.

Doesn't put me off my determination to get a ring on Lilah's finger. There aren't any jewelry stores on the island and I'm trying to think if I have something stashed away that would do, even temporarily. I certainly don't have any traditional engagement rings lying around. Although the band did go through a glam phase early on and maybe there's something in the spare room I use for random shit.

When we sit down for dinner, it feels more like a dinner party than it ever has. It's easy enough to forget what brought additional guests to the table, except for once I actually miss Roman nattering on about his vegetables.

"So, who's watering his precious garden?" I ask Lottie.

She rolls her eyes. "The rabbits cleared it out last week. There's nothing left to water. He'll survive."

I grimace, thinking it might be a close call. There's only three things that Roman is really protective of, Lottie, more recently Sylvie once he knew about her existence, and his damn garden.

Lilah clears her throat nervously. Immediately my attention is diverted to her.

"Sooo, we were wondering and you never really did answer this before..."

Uh oh. "How come you're covered in tattoos in all the official PR shots but you don't actually have any?" Lilah blushes slightly, and I can just imagine how that conversation went. I'd put money on her confirming that she's seen everything there is to see, without even being aware that she said it.

Karl and Ernie start snickering, but let it taper off when I glare at them. "I'm allergic or something. The small one I tried when I was seventeen landed me in the hospital and I was told to steer clear. I get temporary ones made up. They last for a couple of weeks, so good enough for whatever we need to do for publicity."

It's not a big deal, although it felt like it as a teenager. Like I was doomed to be the wimpy one that couldn't even get a tattoo. So I'm surprised to see Lilah frowning at me like she's concerned. I raise an inquiring eyebrow, not ready to alert everyone that she's got something on her mind.

"I think you should stop doing things that don't suit you," she says quietly, but with an air of wisdom that has me sitting back and contemplating her. Apparently, age really is just a number in Lilah's case. But I'm not sure I'm ready to reveal that much of my true self to the general public.

"We can talk about it when Roman's back," I tell her and the others. Karl and Ernie both look dumbfounded.

LILAH

I guess there's comfort in numbers and it's nice to have some additional women to balance out the testosterone. Still, I wish Lance had stayed. He really is like a pouty little brother who's kicking his toe in the dirt. I tried to reason with him, but amazingly, I couldn't get a word out of him. He just firmed his lips and shook his head.

For the first time since I met him, he wasn't the laid-back guy I've seen, even when LuLu was busy starting fires. Maybe once I get to know her better, I can get more information out of Sylvie. Yes, I know it's none of my business, but they're both clearly hurting from something, so if I can fix that…

Lottie keeps looking at her phone anxiously, and I finally figure out that she's waiting to hear from Roman. I can tell when it happens because her shoulders drop about ten inches and her smile lights up her entire face, freckles and all. "Roman will be here in the morning," she announces to no one in particular.

There's a sort of group sigh of relief. Then Todd speaks quietly. "I'll get the downstairs room ready for him. I'm assuming he shouldn't be doing stairs?"

Lottie nods softly. "Is there a cot or something I can move in there? I think I should stay with him for a few nights, at least until he's able to move around on his own." She looks so anxious nobody has the heart to point out that the king-size bed is more than adequate for two. And the way Roman was talking before LuLu came on the scene, he wouldn't object to sharing it with her in the slightest.

Instead, Todd nods with only the slightest twitch to his lips. "There's an armchair in there that pulls out into a twin bed. It was pushed on me for any young children that might visit, but it's a decent size. Will that do?"

Lottie nods enthusiastically. And with that, the after-dinner, lounging-around-the-table scene breaks up.

I head upstairs with Sylvie to find her one of the empty guestrooms. Amazingly, there aren't too many left. "So it looks like there's either the smaller one at the head of the stairs or the one Lance has been using. Your choice," I say as softly as I can, watching her face for any clues. She looks torn, her face has a yearning on it when she stares at the closed door to Lance's room. But then her spine stiffens and her lips tighten briefly. "The small room will be fine. I wouldn't want Lance to feel he has to burn all his possessions."

Ouch. I help her check that the room has everything she needs. It's the only one that doesn't have an ensuite bathroom, so I show her where the main one is on the floor and then say goodnight.

I'm desperate for a shower after sniffing my shirt as I pull it over my head. I'm surprised nobody sent me in here for one before sitting down to dinner. Ugh. That small house was packing a lot of dust and mildew.

My eyes are closed as I let the rainfall shower heads mist my entire body in warm water. I don't even have to turn around. I can just stand here and imagine I'm in some tropical jungle (without any bugs). I'm so lost in my fantasy I yelp when two large hands cup my breasts, taking their weight before two disembodied thumbs roll over my nipples.

Todd chuckles softly against my neck. "Just me, Lilah. No, don't turn around. I'm going to scrub every inch of your sweet body and then I'm planning to fuck you dry." My mouth opens to inquire how he plans to do that. But it snaps shut with a tiny moan when he traces the curve of my hip with an old-fashioned wash cloth. The man is full of surprises.

He stays behind me the entire time, simply reaching around to my front as he follows whatever plan he clearly has laid out in his head. When I swear he's gone over every inch at least twice, he finally growls in my ear. "Lean forward and put your hands on the wall."

That's it. Just one direct order. I fold my arms over my chest. "There wasn't even a please in there," I complain, wanting to turn around to make my point clear with a friendly glare. But once again his hands are on my shoulders, preventing me from turning.

His response is simply a grunt of disapproval.

I contemplate my options. Todd isn't holding me so tight I couldn't step away if I wanted to, it's not that. He's making it clear that those are my two choices. Lean forward or walk away. I'm tempted to prove a point, but in this particular instance do I really want to? I like when he takes charge, at least in the bedroom (or the shower, I guess). And I very much want his cock, currently poking me in the small of my back, deep inside of me where I can properly appreciate it. But I don't want to just give in either. How can I turn the tables here just a little?

An evil grin lights my face, but there aren't any mirrors in here, so Todd can't see it. As I bend forward per his instructions, I reach out and hit the control button that changes the water pattern from rain to stinging sleet without the ice — for now. I debated turning the water temperature down, but I'm not that cruel. Not yet anyway. Without another word, Todd slides into me with one long stroke. His cock is hot and heavy, stretching me wide. I whimper with need. Once again Todd remains still, even when I clamp down on his cock, desperate to sooth the ache building in my body. He waits, his breathing only slightly faster than normal, until I can't take it anymore.

"Todd, please!" I cry out when my nipples feel hard enough to cut glass. Like I've hit a button, he comes to life with a roar, his hands gripping my hips as he pounds into me. In seconds I'm quaking and pressing my palms into the granite tile of the shower, trying to dispel some of the energy spasming down my nerve endings.

I slump forward, only to be caught in protective hands while Todd's cum runs down my thighs and mixes with the water. He tenderly scoops me up and rinses me off before shutting off the shower and stepping out of the enclosure. Despite his earlier promises, he runs a towel slowly over my curves. But so tenderly that I can feel my eyes growing heavy and my muscles reaching for new levels of relaxation.

There aren't any bones left in my body when Todd tucks me up against his side in the bed, still naked, and pulls the covers over us. I'll take up the matter of his high-handedness in the morning. And after I've figured out how to address his most likely point that we both enjoyed the results. A lot.

21

TODD

This is a first. I wake up with my face mashed into my pillow. That part isn't particularly unusual. The way my lips are stretched wide in a smile is what takes me by surprise. My eyes still closed, I assess the situation. I'm comfortable enough, warm and dry, not particularly hungry but something… ah. Lilah.

As I come awake her presence at my back registers more fully. I raise my head to turn it but her soft hands press firmly on my shoulders. "What are you doing?" I mumble into my pillow, curious but still quite content. Although now her light touches on my sides and back are starting to interest my cock too.

"Trying to find your ticklish spot," she mutters with frustration.

I roll onto my side careful not to send her over onto the floor. "I don't have one," I inform her mildly, lying through my teeth.

She sits back on her knees her bare breasts swaying and riveting my gaze.

"Everyone has one, at least one. Somewhere." She eyes my feet with interest. I tuck them out of her reach.

"Nope." Before she can restart her quest I need to distract her. "You have a decision to make, sweetness."

That got her attention. Her eyes go wide and she leans down. "What?"

"If you want to stick to your rule from yesterday that there's no sex before coffee then we need to get up. Now. Otherwise..." I leave the threat (or promise) hanging in the air.

Lilah's face is all curiosity. "Really? Are you just messing with me in a poor attempt at distraction?" She pulls the sheets back to see for herself. I swear my cock hardens into steel under her gaze. She bites her lip. "It would be a shame for that to go to waste," she muses as if to herself but the glint of pure devilment in her eyes has me tugging her down and under me.

Her only protest is a shriek of laughter that I swiftly turn into a moan of pleasure as I kiss her with everything I've got. While my lips and tongue keep her brain occupied, I tease her gently with fingers that hover over her entrance, dancing but never landing for long until her legs start to writhe in an effort to hold my hand still. I pull back just far enough to ask, "Who are you marrying in five days, Lilah?"

My fingers are poised and all of me is still while the sun breaks across her face in a wide smile. "You!" She reaches up to hug my neck and tug me down at the same time.

"Damn right," I respond with satisfaction sinking two fingers into her heat, watching as her face switches to surprise and her body begins to hum.

Before her orgasm dies away completely I slide into her, my cock practically throbbing with joy at being home. Her back arches and her hands flutter on my shoulders. "All of you. I want *all* of you," she mumbles. She's tight, her engorged pussy gripping hard so I pull back. Sliding my hand up her inner thigh I press out lightly widening her entrance and sink into her depths.

My voice is ragged with need when I finally get out the words, "Love you, Lilah."

I'm assuming her response of "Mprrhyh," is encouragement for more as there's a slightly desperate tinge to it. That's twice she's made me smile before we're even out of bed this morning. I double down on my mission to show her what she means to me. My cock slides in and out of her eagerly, picking up speed and increasing the friction until she finally screams my name.

LILAH

Oh, my God. I screamed. At least three times. Possibly loud enough to be heard downstairs. Definitely on the second floor if anyone is still in their rooms.

Todd laughs at me as he runs the bath puff lightly over my curves in the shower while I mumble to myself in horror. "Relax, sweetness. They'll just be grateful for you saving me from being a grumpy bastard. I doubt they'll mention it. Much."

I give him the evil side eye because I can tell he doesn't believe his own words. We need to get the contractors into the little stone cottage stat. And make sure they add extra sound proofing, just in case. The last thing I need is Bethany hearing that. I shudder at the thought, knowing she'd never stop grinning and that I need to call her because I haven't seen her to fill her in on what's happened since that day I thought I'd ruined everything.

Todd practically has to tug me out of the bedroom and downstairs. I tried to barter for him to bring breakfast up (so that maybe everyone would leave the house and I could postpone the inevitable). But he informed me that he didn't want me getting my fill of him until *after* we were married. At least he forgot to try to carry me so that's some progress.

Reluctantly I follow him downstairs almost expecting a gallery of onlookers waiting. But nobody is at the bottom of the stairs and the scene that greets us in the kitchen has nothing to do with being fucked. Well, not the good kind anyway.

Lottie is standing at the kitchen island her fingers nervously tapping the counter while Karl is on one of the landline phones talking in the sternest voice I've heard out of him yet.

Todd asks Lottie quietly, "What's up?"

She raises her head and I can see tears welling at the corner but she's holding it all in. "Roman isn't answering his phone."

"Maybe it ran out of juice?" he asks her softly, almost hopefully.

Karl ends his call and says grimly, "The ambulance service can't get a response either. They last made contact about fifteen miles from the mainland ferry terminal."

EPILOGUE

TODD

Four years later

I owe my sweet and adorable wife revenge for the birthday party she threw me two months ago.

How she managed to arrange the whole thing without me even getting a whiff of it, I don't know. But when we pull up to the new community center at the old air base, I walk into an ordinary event room that's been transformed. Unfortunately not into a private lounge with good scotch and deep seats. No, it's now a quintessential common room of a retirement home, complete with walkers, wheelchairs, and games of canasta all ready to go at the folding tables.

"You trying to make a point?" I ask her dryly as I survey the room already occupied by my friends, all dressed in button front sweaters while leaning on canes. I wasn't dreading turning fifty before this, but now I'm wondering what else she has in store.

Her response is simply to wiggle her eyebrows and grin.

"I don't see any nurses that can hold a candle to you, baby, so I think you're stuck with me." I'm still never going to let her live that down.

"Dang. I knew I was forgetting something!" Lilah laughs, and tugs me over to a table piled high with gag gifts. I spy an analog phone with giant buttons and an electric eyebrow trimmer. I'm eyeing that last one with an odd fascination when my wife (I still can't get enough of calling her that) tugs on my arm again.

"Relax. Everything is going to your uncle and his friends under the guise of recycling from the party," she whispers.

I nod. That actually makes sense. Uncle Lou has only gotten more stubborn and cantankerous as the years go by.

And now with that party fresh in my mind, it's our wedding anniversary and I'm going to get my own back. It took me a long while to figure out the perfect gift, but now that I know what it is, I'm a man possessed. Except that we moved into the new house six months ago and I still can't find anything.

That's partly my fault for not unpacking beyond taking things out of boxes and stuffing them in drawers. But somehow christening each room of the new house and making memories of Lilah moaning on each new piece of furniture seemed more important at the time. Still does, if I'm honest, realizing that I've yet to fuck her on the desk. It's the same desk from the old house, the one she first wrote those sentences on, but we should definitely revisit it for old time's sake.

After I finalize her gift. I find what I'm looking for in the third drawer of the filing cabinet, next to the sale agreement between Lilah and Lance for the coffee shop. I roll my eyes at that one. She should have charged him twice as much.

Then I sit down at the desk and call my lawyer. He curses me out in both English and Spanish when he hears my request. I point out to him that there never was a prenup, so it doesn't need to be modified and why does he care, anyway? Then I pace the width of the room as I wait for him to send over the necessary paperwork to sign.

Finally, an hour later, I slide the final document, which I printed out on thick cardstock just for the occasion, into a plain manila envelope.

LILAH

Isn't it odd that marriage to Todd has turned into my career? And not in a 1950s housewife kind of way. It turned out my flippant words about giving away his money were prophetic because I'm now running not one but *three* charities to do exactly that.

It's a full-time job because donations keep pouring in and I feel responsible for making sure every penny makes a difference the way the donor intended. I love every minute of it. He still has millions, so I'm not in any danger of truly running the well dry.

I love Todd even more than when we first got together, so I'm bracing myself for whatever he has planned for our anniversary. Teaching him how to tease and enjoy life has been my other full-time occupation, and he's slowly letting his grumpy side soften up — a little. He still worries, but maybe only half as much. I want him to have his moment, so I kept my gifts to the relatively conventional. The official gift category for a four-year anniversary is fruit and flowers. So I asked Roman to give me a list of supplies and seeds to start our first vegetable garden in the spring behind our new house — which is the most beautiful thing ever, by the way.

Todd may roll his eyes when he sees my gift, but I have a feeling he'll enjoy having another creative outlet. Plus, he can then give Roman shit more easily. Or maybe they'll team up against the other three.

Now, the small table in the curve of the bedroom window is set and I just need to bring in dinner. Naturally, that's when Todd appears in the doorway frowning and carrying the tray loaded with covered dishes.

"You weren't planning on carrying this up yourself, were you?"

"Ummm. Yes?" I point to the tray stand I'd already moved into the room for just this purpose.

"Lilah. Do we need to go over your lessons about safety on the stairs?" He sets the tray down and pulls me into his arms.

My body tingles at the thought of all his 'lessons' and I smirk. "Maybe?"

"Fuck. We're going to have to move again, into something one story." He's grumbling, but I can tell he doesn't really mean it.

"Anyway, it's your own damn fault if your gift is wrinkled." He hands me a manila envelope. I'm a little surprised. I don't know what I was expecting, but somehow not anything that would fit into a folder.

"Uh. Should I open it now?"

He shrugs casually but his eyes are twinkling diabolically. Now my curiosity is in overdrive.

"Sure, why not?" he drawls.

I pull back the metal brad and open the flap. There's just one single piece of thick paper, so it's not some big legal document. I pull it out and scan it. Then go back to the top and read it over again more carefully, my mouth hanging open. "You didn't," I finally gasp.

"Oh, I did. You should start getting checks in about thirty days." Todd sounds inordinately proud of himself. The document I'm still clenching in my fingers? It's the rights to *that* song. The one I still can't listen to without wincing, and that somehow marked the true start of our relationship. Apparently I now own it.

Todd is watching me carefully, waiting for my reaction, and I don't want to disappoint him. I certainly don't have to put on an act with him, ever. I narrow my eyes and mutter ominously, "Christmas is coming."

Thank you for reading!

If you're not ready to say goodbye to Todd and Lilah, there's a bonus scene for your ereader here (**https:// BookHip.com/JMSRGBZ**) explaining how Lilah ended up front and center on the band's next album cover - not at all what she had planned!

The *Everyday Famous* series continues with Roman's story. If you love to track characters between books, Todd first appeared in *Challenging Burke* and the architect William Zver has an extra steamy holiday romance in *Her Christmas Beast!*

Find more fun details and books on my website:
https://oliviasinclairbooks.com

About Olivia Sinclair

I write lighthearted steamy romance featuring alphalicious heroes who know what they want and strong, smart heroines that can spot gold underneath a rough exterior.

My promise to you: no cheating, always an HEA, and more than a few silly bits!

I love my characters and I want them all to live happily ever after (along with fabulous careers, chubby babies, and/or adorable pets). Sometimes this requires letting go of how the real world works. I'm okay with that and I hope you are too!

I live and work in the wilds of the Pacific Northwest where I like to experiment with making wine and sourdough bread when I'm not writing or being lectured by my adorably entitled chickens.